Clint Dawson explains how a "chauffeur" became a modern-day Cyrano....

"After Shannon admitted in an interview that she'd always wanted to receive romantic love letters, it seemed like every lowlife who could afford a first-class stamp was writing to the 'lonely heiress.'

"Now, my *real* job—though she doesn't know it—is protecting her from people like that. So I thought *I'd* try sending her letters—to make her happy, and to keep her safe....

"And it turned out writing love letters wasn't all that hard. Because there's something else Shannon doesn't know about me—that I've been in love with her for a long, long time. All I had to do was put down on paper what has always been in my heart...."

Dear Reader,

Well, I'm no heiress—would that I were! But after entering the dating fray, I can see why Shannon Powell, heroine of Maris Soule's *Heiress Seeking Perfect Husband*, would try a new tack: telling a reporter exactly what she's looking for. Of course, I doubt I'd get any letters as wonderful as those Shannon gets from "Cyrano." I also doubt my letter writer would turn out to be my handsome, in-love-with-me-for-forever chauffeur. Of course, maybe that's because I don't have a chauffeur, and because the men who drive me home are more likely to think Cyrano comes from Syria than that he's a lover straight out of literature. But that's another story!

And so is this: Lori Herter's *Me? Marry You?* This is the latest in her MILLION-DOLLAR MARRIAGES miniseries, and it's a winner. I mean, really, who could turn down an all-expense-paid vacation with *the* most gorgeous hunk? Not Penelope Grey, even though she knows the hunk's over-the-top-wealthy father is angling to make a match between them. In fact, before too long, Penelope is hoping gorgeous Craig Derring will fall right in line with those incredibly romantic plans.

So enjoy both of this month's books, and don't forget to come back next month for more great reading about meeting, dating—and marrying!—Mr. Right.

Leslie Wainger

Leslie Wainger
Senior Editor and Editorial Coordinator

Please address questions and book requests to:
Silhouette Reader Service
U.S.: 3010 Walden Ave., P.O. Box 1325, Buffalo, NY 14269
Canadian: P.O. Box 609, Fort Erie, Ont. L2A 5X3

MARIS SOULE

Heiress Seeking Perfect Husband

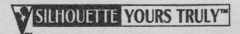

SILHOUETTE YOURS TRULY™

Published by Silhouette Books

America's Publisher of Contemporary Romance

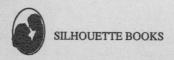 SILHOUETTE BOOKS

ISBN 0-373-52036-0

HEIRESS SEEKING PERFECT HUSBAND

Copyright © 1997 by Maris Soule

Printed in U.S.A.

About the author

Ah, to be able to write beautiful prose and win the heart of the one you love. The first time I read *Cyrano de Bergerac,* I fell in love with the story. Here was a man with a big nose (bigger than big), in love with Roxanne. He could tell her of his love in the shadows of night under the guise of being someone else and through letters, but not in person. The story was funny, romantic and tragic. What a great idea for a contemporary romance! In *Heiress Seeking Perfect Husband,* Shannon Powell nearly overlooks the man who loves her. Maybe he doesn't have a big nose, but he certainly doesn't see himself as a suitor.

Love letters have always meant a lot to me. Twenty-nine years ago, a redhead with blue eyes sent love letters to me. The red is now fading from his hair, but his eyes are as blue and he's still writing me love notes. See? The ending doesn't always have to be tragic....

Books by Maris Soule

Silhouette Yours Truly

Heiress Seeking Perfect Husband

Silhouette Romance

1

—→ ←—

"Have you gotten to it yet?"

Shannon Powell looked up from her bowl of cereal and the Sunday edition of the *Detroit News and Free Press*. Her chauffeur stood on the opposite side of the mahogany dining table, his muscular arms crossed in front of his broad chest. The gesture stretched the fabric of his blue blazer to its limit, while a dark scowl etched creases across his forehead.

"Gotten to what?" she asked. Clint Dawson had been driving her around Grosse Pointe and the Detroit suburbs for three years. He usually checked with her in the morning to see what her plans were for the day, but rarely did he bother her during breakfast, and never had he sounded so accusing.

"To the 'Metro' section," he said, nodding at the newspaper on the table. "The article about you is in there."

She turned to the section and saw the problem. How could she miss it? Smack-dab in the center of the page was her picture...and right below was the headline Heiress Wants Love Letters.

Immediately Shannon looked up at Clint. "How could she?"

He raised his eyebrows. *"She?"*

"The reporter. All through the interview, she assured me that this would be an article about the painting. How could she put *that* in?"

"You didn't say it?"

"What I said was John never wrote me love letters. It was an offhanded remark. The interview was over, and she was putting away her notebook and tape recorder. My comment should have been off the record."

Clint scoffed. "With reporters, nothing's 'off the record.' You should know that by now. What led you to say something like that?"

"I..." She stopped herself. She'd goofed, but she wasn't going to make excuses. "That is my business."

"And my business is to..."

He didn't finish. A muscle in his jaw twitched and his arms dropped to his sides. She cocked her head. "Yes...? Your business is to what, Clint?"

She watched him take in a breath. "My business," he answered, his voice level, "is to drive you places, to tend to your vehicles and to oversee the estate's security systems."

And to watch over her, she was certain, though John had assured her that wasn't why he'd hired Clint. "He's here to drive you anywhere you want to go when I'm not available and to make sure no one breaks in and steals my works of art," he'd explained.

She'd needed a chauffeur three years ago. Still needed one. Being afraid to drive was crazy, but try as she might, she couldn't get up the nerve to sit behind the wheel. Just thinking about it brought back memories of the accident.

She had her suspicions, however, that Clint was more than her chauffeur. "I don't need a bodyguard," she said firmly.

"I'm sure you don't." Clint didn't look away. She might not think she needed a bodyguard, but he knew better.

Clint kept his expression guarded and concentrated on her eyes. From the first time he'd met her, he'd found her eyes fascinating. Normally a warm blue, whenever she was upset, they turned dark and cloudy. They were sapphire at the moment, sparkling with curiosity. Sometimes he wondered what color her eyes turned when she was aroused.

Not that he would ever know.

As he'd expected, Shannon gave in first, looking back down at the paper, her hair falling like a silken veil of pale gold by the side of her face. "Damn, but I hate people who lie," she muttered.

Which kept him in a precarious position. She might suspect he was watching out for her, but as long as she wasn't certain, she wouldn't do anything. He had to live a lie or lose his job.

"I told the paper I didn't give personal interviews." Shannon kept her gaze on the page. "This was only supposed to be about the Rembrandt and the reception. I wouldn't have talked to that reporter otherwise."

"Which I'm sure they knew," Clint said. "And the woman covered herself. The information about the painting and reception is there... in the last paragraph. It's the paragraphs leading up to there that go into how you're looking for a husband."

Again her head snapped up, her hair cascading in soft waves back to her shoulders. "I never said I was looking for a husband."

"That's the way she's made it sound."

"All I said was, 'I *probably* would remarry.'"

"And you should. John's been dead for over a year now... you're twenty-seven..." And from what his sister had told him, a woman's sex drive increased in her late twenties. "It's just that a woman in your financial position should not be advertising for a husband in the newspaper."

"I am not advertising."

"You did ask for love letters."

"No I didn't! All I said was John never sent me any, and I—"

She didn't finish, and he knew what she'd said. "That you would like some?"

"Okay, so I said I would like to get a love letter. I meant someday. Not now." Again Shannon looked down at the article, quickly scanning its contents. As Clint had said, the facts about her donating the Rembrandt to the Detroit Art Institute in John's memory and the ceremony and reception that would be held that afternoon were there, at the end. Everything else leading up to that paragraph, however, was personal.

Right away, the story reminded readers that ten years ago she'd married multimillionaire John Powell, to the surprise of many. Few had thought the forty-two-year-old confirmed bachelor would ever marry, much less marry a woman twenty-five years his junior—a child just out of high school and definitely not of his social class.

No one had been more surprised than she.

What she's looking for in a man. The words were in bold print and clearly made it sound as if she were on a manhunt. A list of criteria followed.

Shannon looked up. "I never gave her any list of things I was looking for in a man."

Clint moved around the table to stand by her side. She caught a whiff of his after-shave when he leaned closer to glance at the paper. The scent was stronger than any John had used, muskier. But then, there were few similarities between the two men.

Clint was tall, brawny and imposing. With his thick brown hair and dark brown eyes, he reminded her of a big grizzly bear. Debonair had described John, along with quiet and intellectual. The first time she saw him come into Mabel's Diner, he'd made her think of a silver fox.

He was a man who'd been born to money. Urbane and sophisticated, he'd taken over the family business when his father had died. He'd traveled to countries all over the world, had dined with royalty and important dignitaries. His schooling had been the best, his manners were perfect and Shannon had been stunned the day he asked her to marry him.

Clint was the type she'd thought she would end up with. Rough around the edges described him. Articulate, but certainly not sophisticated, and she had a feeling he didn't care. Clint's past was less than perfect, according to what John had told her. John had also said a man who could break into a house would know how to keep others out.

He'd trusted Clint. She hadn't. Not at first, at least.

Actually, when she looked back on it, she'd acted quite childish when John hired Clint. She would like to have blamed her behavior on the pain she was in at the time, but the truth was, he'd scared her. Only slowly had she learned to trust him. Over time, she'd discovered the rough exterior hid a gentle core, and when John had died, Clint was the one she'd leaned on. He was there whenever she needed him—a solid rock willing to listen to her reminisce late into the night. In a way, they'd become friends, and there were times she felt very much at ease with Clint. Then again, there were times, like this moment, when his nearness was disquieting.

She glanced up at his face and found him looking at her. Quickly he turned back to the paper. "It seems a bit ridiculous," he said, "to put 'Money not important' at the top of the list. In your position, why would it be?"

Shannon looked back at the article. "Actually, I told her money's never been important to me, not even when I married John."

He pointed at the next item on the list. "Age makes no difference?"

"She asked if, when I remarried, it would be to another older man. I told her I thought there were more important things to consider than a man's age."

Straightening, Clint stepped back. "Things like love letters?"

It was the sarcasm she heard that she responded to. "And what's wrong with wanting love letters? Love letters are a gift from the soul, something a woman can cherish for years to come." Sadly, John simply hadn't been a man of many words, verbal or written.

"I'm not saying there's anything wrong with a woman wanting love letters," Clint argued. "It's telling the world that you want them. Do you realize you are now going to have every con man and charlatan in town writing to you?"

Her chin came up in defiance. "So let them write. Where are they going to send these letters? My address isn't mentioned, and I'm not listed in the phone book."

"And how many 'block-long walled-in estates on Lake Erie' do you think there are in Grosse Pointe?" he asked, quoting straight from the article. "They'll find ways of getting the letters to you. You'll have more proposals than you know what to do with."

"Okay, then, what do you suggest I do about it?" Again she glanced at the paper. "I can't make this go away."

"Let me go through your mail when it comes. I can take care of any letters you get before you even see them."

"You'd go through my mail?"

"For a few weeks at least. Until this blows over."

It would make it easy for her. She could let him handle everything, let him deal with the problem. Just like she'd let John deal with all of her problems, just like she was still letting Clint deal with her fear of driving.

Shannon shook her head. "No. It's time I start taking control of my life."

"This isn't about control," Clint insisted.

"Yes it is." It was about control and growing up, and making her own decisions. She grinned. "Besides, I might find some of the letters interesting."

"Is that what you're looking for?" His tone was accusing. "A little entertainment?"

She bristled. "Of course not."

"Then . . . ?"

Flipping her hair back from her face, Shannon looked Clint straight in the eye. "You've made your point about the letters, but I'll be the one who decides what to do with them. That is, if I get any. Now, is there anything else you wanted to discuss?"

Clint knew there was a lot more he wanted to discuss, but nothing more he could say. How did you protect a woman who didn't want protecting? How did you stop wanting what you could never have? "What time should I have the car ready this afternoon?" he asked.

"Two o'clock would be fine," she said and went back to her bowl of cereal and the paper.

She'd dismissed him, and quite efficiently. What a change from the woman he'd met his first year on the job. Shannon had been twenty-five then, but still a child. The whiplash she'd sustained when her car was rear-ended had been part of her problem, but mostly she hadn't grown up. John hadn't wanted her to grow up. He'd kept her a child, doing her thinking for her, planning her day and her life. He simply hadn't planned his death.

Thrown on her own, Shannon Powell was turning into one very stubborn female who wasn't going to let anyone tell her what to do. The child had become a woman.

And somewhere along the way he'd fallen in love with her. Turning away, he walked out of the dining room.

That afternoon, standing unobtrusively in the background, Clint watched Shannon as she officially presented the Rembrandt to the Art Institute's director. Compared to most of the other women present, she was a breath of spring air on a cold afternoon in April. Sometimes awkward, ever enthusiastic and always open and forthright, she was a masterpiece in her own right, and he could understand why John Powell had fallen in love with her and had worried about her. Clint could still remember his last lengthy conversation with John. It had been the day he'd turned in his resignation.

"You can't quit," John had insisted. "She's as innocent as a kitten and won't believe anyone would harm her."

"You should tell her what happened," Clint had argued. "She needs to know."

With a shake of his head, John had dismissed that suggestion. "The experience has scared her out of driving. I don't want her scared to step out the door. As long as you're watching over her, why tell her?"

"That's the point," Clint had insisted. "I can't keep acting as her bodyguard. I have a business to get started. When you hired me, I told you I could only do this for two years."

"But how am I going to replace you?" John had asked. "It took her a while, but now she trusts you. Someone else might not be able to pull off this little deception."

"What about Angelo?"

Again John had objected. "Angelo's a good enough replacement on your days off, but I wouldn't trust him all the time. No, Angelo is happy as my gardener, and that's where he should stay."

"Then you've got to find someone to take my place."

Reluctantly John had sighed. "Will you promise to stay on and protect her until I do find a replacement?"

Clint had promised he would...and two days later, John Powell had dropped dead of a heart attack.

He couldn't leave then, not with Shannon as devastated as she had been. He knew too well what she was going through. And though it had been money that had initially prompted his decision to take the job, his reasons for staying on, month after month, grew to be far more complex...or perhaps very simple.

He fell in love with her, and just as John had wanted her protected, so did he. A part of him would die if anything happened to her.

Clint watched Shannon walk across the room to talk to Paul Green, John's longtime friend and financial adviser. She'd pulled her hair back into a twist but a few strands had already come loose and hung by the side of her face. Ever so often she pushed one back, only to have it slip out again. Paul said something, and Shannon laughed, the sound rippling through the gallery.

"What *is she* trying to prove?"

The question caught him off guard, and Clint looked to his right. A tall blonde in her mid- to late forties had come up beside him. She was looking directly at Shannon. "Look at her," the woman grumbled. "She's after Paul now. Not that I'm surprised. After all, any woman who advertises in the paper that she wants a husband—"

Clint interrupted. "She didn't say that."

"Didn't she?" the woman asked, not sounding a bit like she believed him and waving a hand toward two men standing by the newly donated Rembrandt. "Those two can't wait to get their letters written. You ought to have heard what they said."

Clint studied the pair she'd indicated. Their suits looked tailor-made, they were well-groomed and in their late thirties. Successful businessmen. Men with good educations, culture and money. He looked back at the woman. "What did they say?"

"That they'd be more than happy to marry her."

The woman snorted and Clint smiled. Perhaps that article was going to work out all right. He couldn't keep on working for Shannon, not the way he felt. He didn't trust himself. One day he might forget himself and act on his desires. One day he might show her how he felt, and that would be a mistake.

If she knew he was in love with her, she would probably have hysterics, laugh herself silly. To think a woman as beautiful as Shannon might be interested in him was pushing it. And even if she didn't reject the idea, it still wouldn't work. He wasn't right for her. He represented what she'd risen above. He was beer and baseball, motorcycles and leather. John had given her champagne and the ballet, yachts and silk.

No, he couldn't let her know how he felt. What he had to do was hope she found someone right for her, someone who would watch over her. Then, Clint knew, he could get on with his life.

Monday evening, Clint changed his mind about the virtues of the article. Every Monday night, after spending a few hours at the community center in his old neighborhood, he stopped by The Grill on Mack Avenue. The Grill attracted a diverse crowd, most of its regulars being singles who worked at nearby companies and stopped by for a bite to eat before heading home. Initially Clint had thought he might meet some women there. What he'd ended up doing was learning a lot about computers.

Why Gary Cleveland had decided to latch on to him was beyond Clint. They had nothing in common. Intellectually, Gary was probably a genius; socially, he was a nerd. Of course, to hear Gary talk, he was soon to be elected Playboy of the year.

This evening, Gary arrived after Clint had already seated himself at a table. Short, slightly pudgy, balding and wearing glasses, Gary came through the door, looked around the restaurant, then walked straight toward Clint's table. Grinning like a Cheshire cat, he pulled out a chair and sat down. "So how goes it?"

"Not bad." Clint knew something was up.

Still grinning, Gary leaned back in his chair. "I hear your boss lady is looking for a husband."

He said it loud enough for others in the restaurant to hear and look up, and Clint cringed. "She's not looking for a husband," he grumbled and reached for his glass of water. "That was a misquote."

Gary wasn't to be deterred. "The headline said she wants love letters."

"When she decides to remarry. That's not going to happen for a while."

"That's not the way I read it. Or the others."

"Others?" Clint didn't like the sound of that.

"The other guys at Braxton's." Gary grinned, sitting straight again. "At least those of us who don't have wives. We've got a bet on whose letter she'll answer first, and if one of us can get her to go out, he wins a weekend at the Renaissance Center, all expenses paid."

Clint was sure Gary expected to be cashing in on the weekend. His short size and excess poundage had never held him back from hustling women in the restaurant. Panache was the man's middle name.

Not that Clint thought Gary would have any more success with Shannon than he had had with the women in the restaurant.

"What about you?" Gary asked. "You going to write her love letters?"

"Me?" He'd never even considered the possibility. "Don't be ridiculous."

"It wouldn't be the first time a society chick ran off with the chauffeur."

"Shannon—Mrs. Powell—is no chick, and she wouldn't be interested in this chauffeur." He didn't want her interested in him.

"Then how about writing a love letter for me?" Gary asked.

"You?"

Gary shrugged as if it didn't matter, but the nervous way he kept shifting his weight in his chair gave him away. "Letter writing isn't one of my fortes. Give me any computer at Braxton's, and I can create a program that will write love letters galore. Only problem is, the prose it kicked out wouldn't be worth the paper it was printed on. What I need is a little creative assistance. Your assistance."

"And what makes you think I could do a better job than you?"

"You know her... know her likes and dislikes. You write those stories for those dropouts you're teaching to read."

"Those stories are at a third- and fourth-grade reading level, about life on the streets. I don't think Shannon would be overly impressed."

"You went to college. You had to write papers."

"On criminal justice."

"All I'm asking for are a few mushy sentences. Something that turns her on."

"No," Clint said firmly.

"Hey, you owe me," Gary reminded him. "Didn't I help you with the security system on her place?" A muscle along the side of his face twitched. "Didn't I get you a computer for your mother?"

Clint knew then that asking Gary for help had been a mistake. A few tips on how to devise a computerized security system and one computer for his mother—used, but in good working order—were now going to cost him.

"I just want to get a letter back from her. That's all," Gary insisted. "I mean, how would it look if Gary Cleveland didn't get a letter and all the other guys did?"

Clint wasn't sure he cared, but paybacks were paybacks. With a sigh, he gave in. "All right, I'll write your damn letter."

Tuesday, Shannon knew she'd underestimated the readership of the *Detroit News and Free Press*. Clarissa, who'd worked as cook and housekeeper for the Powells ever since John's father had brought her and her husband, Angelo, over from Italy, was muttering when she brought in the day's mail. "So many," she exclaimed. "Is too much."

Shannon agreed. There had to be at least fifty letters mixed in with the usual junk mail and bills.

She went through the pile slowly, stacking the letters according to her impression of each. Some of the addresses were masterpieces in creativity, and how the post office had figured out to send them to her was beyond her reasoning. Others were disturbingly accurate, down to the correct street number.

She picked one with a typed address and slit it open with her letter opener. Cautiously she pulled out the folded paper, not sure what to expect, then laughed. It was an application for a dating service.

That one went into the wastebasket.

Next, she chose one with a hand-written address on a pink envelope. The note inside was only a few lines long.

Shannon,
I saw your pickture in the Sunday paper and think your real pritty. I'm not real good at writing, but I'd like to meet you. You can call me at 555-9654. I got layed off from were I was working, so I'm around most of the time.

Carl

Shannon decided *literate* needed to be added to her list of requirements. Carl also went into the wastebasket.

And so did George, who was "kind of still married, but his wife didn't understand him"; and Chuck, who felt the rich should open their homes to those living on the streets; and Mark, who for three typewritten pages quoted Bible verses regarding love. She was beginning to think she should have let Clint go through the stack. This was really a waste of time. Then she came across one letter that did interest her.

"Dear Shannon," it began, the handwriting a flourish of curved lines.

I feel that we are kindred souls. People no longer appreciate the written word, and letter writing is becoming a lost art. The telephone and computer have replaced the act of putting pen to paper.

But how can one savor the beauty of words if they are spoken then gone? Faxes and E-mail are no more than bytes along the electronic highway, thrown into cyberspace, to be filed or printed with the click of a mouse. A letter, especially a love letter, should be intimate. Personal. It should take effort, and in that effort it becomes the gift of love.

I do not presume to write you a love letter, yet the sight of your face in that newspaper awakened something within my soul. I saw in your eyes a longing for happiness, and I know a longing of my own. So tell me your dreams, and I'll tell you mine and somewhere in time, our souls may meet.

Awaiting your answer.

Gary

Shannon read the letter a second time. "I feel that we are kindred souls." Well, he'd certainly voiced her feelings about faxes and E-mail, and to call a love letter a gift of love...

It was uncanny.

She started to drop the letter into the wastebasket, then changed her mind. Folding it carefully, she slipped it into her pocket.

2

By the end of the week, Shannon had received over one hundred letters. She scanned them all, tossing most. In ten she found something that caught her interest, and those she kept, slipping them into a manila folder on her desk. She wasn't surprised by Clint's reaction when she told him her plans.

"You're going to what?" he demanded.

"Write back," she repeated.

"You know nothing about these men. They could be murderers. Rapists."

"Clint, all I'm going to do is answer their letters. If there's any murdering or raping, it will probably be in my usage of the English language."

"There's nothing wrong with your English," he grumbled.

"That's not what my college English teacher said before I dropped out of her class."

For a moment he hesitated; then he shook his head. "You're changing the subject."

"Because there's nothing to discuss."

"Who are these guys? What are their names?"

She grinned, closed the folder and leaned back in her chair. "Does it matter what their names are? I'm the one writing, not you. You're worse than John ever was."

"Because writing letters to men you don't know could put you in danger. Someone with the kind of money you've inherited—"

"Can enjoy writing to a man just as much as someone without money. I'm going to do this, so end of discussion." She glanced at her watch, then shook her head. "I'm also going to be late for my hair appointment if I don't get going."

Shannon pushed her chair back from the desk and stood. She expected Clint to move away from the doorway. He didn't. Like a stone wall, he blocked her passage, his dark gaze locked on her face.

He was wearing his customary uniform, the blue blazer and gray slacks giving him a polished look. With Clint, the look was superficial. There was no polishing granite.

She stopped a few feet in front of him, lifted her chin and silently issued her challenge.

She could see his chest expand as he took in a deep breath, his jacket tightening across his broad shoulders, and she felt the tension within him. "If John were alive, you wouldn't be doing this."

"No," she agreed. "I wouldn't be. But he's not alive." She was the one who felt alive. Challenging Clint had her adrenaline pumping. Boldly she stepped forward.

Immediately Clint stepped back, his gaze never leaving her face. In his eyes, she saw a guarded look, and when he spoke, his attitude was formal. "Which car will you want? The Mercedes or the Jaguar?"

"The Mercedes," she answered just as formally and walked past him.

It wasn't until she was halfway up the stairs and Clint had gone out to the garage to get the car that she grinned. "Yes!" she proclaimed and raised her fist in victory. She'd faced down Mr. Intimidation, had taken control.

* * *

Monday was Clint's day off, and since going to work for John Powell, he'd developed a set routine. In the morning he ran errands, then around lunchtime, he went over to his mother's. For years he'd been trying to get her to move. The old neighborhood had been a bad place to live when he was growing up, and it was getting worse every day. For years she'd been saying no.

She was as stubborn as they came, and since she wouldn't move, he'd concentrated on making the place as safe and comfortable as he could manage. In the past three years, he'd built a tall wooden fence around the property, had installed an alarm system, central heat and air-conditioning and had bought her a television that got one hundred and fifty channels. He'd also gotten her the computer from Gary.

She usually had one or two chores for him to do when he came by—something to repair or check. She would then feed him lunch and they would talk, and sometimes his sister would stop by with her two children. Mondays were better now than the Mondays he remembered as a child.

Around three, he would head over to the neighborhood community center. No more than a brick building with most of the windows boarded up, in ways it was a second home to Clint. It was there he'd found the guidance he'd needed: Don Williams.

Don was the Center's founder and director. He was a big man, proud of his African heritage and a straight talker. He took no guff, and he believed curing the problems of the neighborhood was everyone's responsibility. A half hour a week was all he asked of people. A half hour to save a child.

Clint openly admitted that if it weren't for Don, he would be in jail or dead. He gave more than a half hour a week. He taught others to read, as Don had taught him; he taught others to wrestle, as he'd once done; and he listened, for he knew the pain.

Leon Washington was Clint's most recent pupil. In a small room off the recreation hall, Clint sat with Leon at a table and listened to the eighteen-year-old high school dropout haltingly sound out the words in the latest story Clint had created. Only when Leon hesitated then looked up, did Clint help him. After three sentences with no stops for assistance, Leon paused in his reading. "Not bad, huh?"

"Great."

"You really stole a tank when you was in Kuwait?"

"Yeah," Clint admitted. The boy's comprehension was improving.

"Ever steal a car?" Leon glanced toward the one unboarded window that faced the street.

"Once when I was twelve." He'd done it to prove to his father that he could. All he'd proven was he was a fool.

"Ever do it ag'in?"

"No, but in the Marines, I..." He smiled, deciding it was best not to say what he'd done in the Marines. "Sometimes one's skills do come in handy."

Leon grinned in understanding, his teeth white against his dark skin. "Maybe I'll join the Marines, like you did. Get me out of this here neighborhood."

"Gotta get your GED first."

"I know. Gettin' better, ain't I?"

"The rate you're going, you'll be reading *War and Peace* in no time."

"I like reading your stories." He glanced at the page on the table. "I could never understand those books them other teachers gave me. But you is one of us. You know how it is."

"I've been there."

"Don told me about you and your brothers. He says one be in Jackson?"

Clint nodded.

"One of the brothers on the street was sent there last week. Got caught for armed robbery. He's in for twenty."

"It's not going to be the Holiday Inn."

"No, that it ain't gonna be." Leon cocked his head quizzically. "How comes you didn't end up like your brothers?"

"Don," Clint answered, nodding in the direction of Don Williams's office. "He taught me I wasn't as tough as I thought, woke me up to the fact that I could make choices."

"I seen your trophies," Leon said. "Seen you wrestling with the other guys. You're tough."

"There's always someone tougher." He'd learned that. "And a bullet can cut down the toughest of us." He'd learned that, too.

Leon nodded and went back to his reading.

On Mondays, Shannon usually stayed home. Clarissa's husband, Angelo, wasn't a bad driver, but Shannon never felt as safe with him as she did with Clint. She used Mondays to update her financial records—a skill she'd had to learn after John's death—pay bills and do some reading.

Around three-thirty, Shannon stepped into the kitchen knowing Clarissa would be there preparing dinner. The middle-aged woman looked up from the potato she was peeling and smiled. "Good afternoon, Meessus Powell," she said. "Is something you need?"

"Something to drink." Shannon waved Clarissa back to her work. "I can get it myself."

Crossing the room, she went to the refrigerator. There she found a bottle of lime-flavored mineral water. After twisting off the cap, she walked over to where Clarissa was working. "Did you and Angelo do anything exciting yesterday?" she asked.

"We went to Mass. Then we visit my cousin Isabella. Her daughter, Maria, is in Italy now. In Torino, where Angelo and I come from. Isabella had a letter from her. With pictures. Things have changed since Angelo and I left."

"I imagine they have. What's it been—thirty years?"

"Thirty-two since your husband's father bring us over to work for him." Clarissa shook her head. "So many years. My children grow up. Meester and Meessus Powell die. Now the younger Meester Powell, he is gone. Is lonely with him gone, yes?"

"It's lonely," Shannon agreed.

"Is a shame you and Meester Powell not blessed with children."

"We tried."

"I know." Clarissa nodded. "He was a good man."

"A very good man."

"But now time to let go, yes? Meester Powell, he would not want you to spend your life alone."

"No, he wouldn't have," she said, though it wasn't something she'd ever discussed with John. "And I am letting go." Of the heartache and sadness. She would always have the memories. "Not that it's easy." Shannon laughed. "Especially with one person in this household who would like to keep me wrapped in a cocoon."

"Clint?" Clarissa asked, stretching out his name as she reached for a bag of carrots.

Shannon nodded. "I swear he's getting more paranoid every day. Like these letters I'm writing. He makes it sound like I'm putting myself in terrible jeopardy just by keeping up a correspondence with ten men."

"He worries about you. Likes you, I think."

"Clint?" He'd certainly never given her any indication. "You're kidding."

Her expression serious, Clarissa shook her head. "No. Sometimes, the way he looks at you..."

Shannon had seen his looks lately. "Don't you mean *scowls* at me?"

"When you looking, maybe. But when you not looking..." Clarissa smiled.

"Really?" That she was pleased surprised Shannon. She hadn't thought she cared. "Has he ever said anything?"

"Him?"

Clarissa laughed, and Shannon understood. Clint was like John in that aspect. The strong, silent type.

"You like him?" Clarissa asked.

Did she like him? Shannon turned the question over in her mind. Yes, she did like Clint. Did she like him in the way Clarissa meant?

She hadn't thought about it before. "I find him interesting." Intriguing. "He certainly helped me after John died." With his quiet support. "He was there when I needed him."

"But no—?" Clarissa patted her chest over her heart.

Accelerated heartbeat? Shannon grinned. "Maybe." There were those stabs of excitement that cut through her at the most unexpected times when he was around.

And though Clint wasn't handsome, he wasn't bad looking, either. In some ways he reminded her of Steven Seagal. He could also be very nice. She'd certainly appreciated his support after John died. She always felt safe around him... protected.

"No," Shannon said, coming to her senses. "Clarissa, you're letting your imagination get away from you." And so had she for a moment. "Clint's not interested in me. Just the other day he was telling me exactly what qualities I should be looking for in a husband. The description certainly didn't fit him."

Clarissa frowned. "I thought you said he wants you not to marry?"

"What he wants is to be the one who does the picking and choosing of my next husband. I'm driving him crazy writing to men he doesn't know. Which reminds me, you did mail those letters I left on the table in the hallway last week, didn't you?"

"I did," Clarissa assured her. "Put them in the box Thursday morning. They should have them by now."

Shannon grabbed one of the carrots Clarissa had just peeled. "Good." She smiled. "I'm curious about how they answer the question I asked."

By four o'clock, Leon had finished the story and had written a short summary. His spelling was terrible, but the ideas were coming together. After Leon left, Clint helped Don get the mats ready for wrestling practice, then he worked out with the two heavyweights Don was sponsoring in the state's freestyle program. After that, he showered and headed for The Grill. Gary was already seated at a table and waved him over.

"I did it!" he said, beaming and holding up an envelope. "She answered. Her letter came Friday. I won the pool at work."

Putting his hands up, Gary did a little wiggle in his chair, rocked it off balance and ended up on the floor with a thud. Clint stood, staring at him, then shaking his head, helped him up. "You okay?"

"Fine. Absolutely fine." Gary grinned, picked up his fallen chair and sat down again. "How sweet it is!"

Clint frowned. So she'd chosen his letter—Gary's letter—to respond to. He wasn't sure if he should be pleased or concerned. It proved she could be swayed by a few flowery lies.

"What?" Gary asked, his grin of triumph switching to a look of concern. "You're frowning. What's wrong? What do you know that I don't know?"

"Nothing," Clint said. "Other than she's answered ten letters."

"And—?"

"And that's all," Clint said. He motioned toward the envelope. "What did she say?"

Gary's grin completely gone, he glanced down at the envelope in his hand. "She said she liked my letter, and that she would like to correspond with me, share ideas...dreams. Then she asked if I thought there was a plan to life or if things just happened?" He looked at Clint. "How in the hell am I supposed to know? I'm a computer programmer, not some damned philosopher."

Clint smiled, pleased with the question. At least she'd been honest when she'd said these wouldn't be love letters. "It's something she's been wondering about since her husband died."

"So what do I say so she'll go out with me?"

"I don't think she's looking for a date, just someone to write to."

"Well, I'm looking for a date. Don't forget, if I get her to go out with me, I win a weekend at the Renaissance Center, all expenses paid." He grinned. "Hell, I might even take her there."

Clint could imagine what a night that would be. Gary would probably fall out of the bed. He started to smile, then stopped himself. He certainly hoped Shannon wasn't so desperate for a man that she would consider sleeping with Gary.

"So what are we going to tell her?" Gary asked.

"We?" Clint frowned.

"About this plan-to-life business," Gary said, glancing down at the envelope.

Clint understood what Gary wanted. "No way," he said, shaking his head. "I wrote the first letter. Now it's up to you."

"You consider a half-page letter equal to hours and hours of my expertise on that security system, not to mention a computer?"

Clint knew then that Gary was going to milk this for all he could. "So how much will equal your assistance and a computer?"

"You'll know," Gary assured him and leaned down to open his briefcase. "I've got some paper. I thought we could get started while we were eating."

Within two weeks, Shannon had received answers to her second batch of letters. One arrived just before she was to leave for a bridge game at the country club. She took it with her.

"Now this is an interesting analogy," she said from the back seat of the Jaguar. " 'Life is a jigsaw puzzle,' this guy writes. 'Too many wrong choices and you can mess up the entire picture. A lost piece will always be missed. Yet even with a mistake here and there, you don't need to throw it away. The parts can become a whole, the total understood.' "

"Life is a jigsaw?" Clint scoffed from the front seat. "Sounds like the bit in *Forrest Gump*, you know the one about life being like a box of chocolates, and you never know what you're going to get."

"Yeah, well, I like the image of a jigsaw puzzle. John was a part of my life and now he's gone. I will miss him, but that doesn't mean I have to stop living—stop working on the entire picture."

"Still sounds pretty corny," Clint said. "Who wrote that?"

"Gary Cle..." She stopped herself, grinning at the back of his head. He'd almost gotten her to tell. "Sneaky, Dawson."

"Just curious."

He didn't look away from the road, and she supposed, in his position, she'd be as curious. "Well, to satisfy your curiosity, this one was written by Gary Cleveland. He was the last of the ten to answer my letters. His came today."

"Just today?" Clint glanced back at her, then quickly faced forward again. "I mean, doesn't it seem like it took this guy a long time to answer?"

"Actually, it's postmarked a week ago Tuesday, but the zip code on the envelope was wrong. I suppose that delayed it."

Clint shook his head. "Doesn't sound like this Gary's very smart."

"Smarter than some of the men who wrote back." She couldn't believe the differences in their second letters. "I got quite an education reading a couple. You'll be pleased to know I've now cut my list down to three. Actually, up until this letter arrived, it was two."

"And what is it about the other two that you liked?"

"Well, one used poetry to answer my questions. He compared life to a highway and people to cars. He said each turnoff takes us in a new direction. Sometimes we take one, then wonder if we should have taken another."

"Robert Frost," Clint said. "'The Road Not Taken.' Two paths... which one to follow?"

"Right." Martin had said he was paraphrasing Frost. "He teaches English at the University of Michigan."

"And your third letter writer?" Clint asked, glancing back as they waited for a stoplight to turn. "What did he have to say?"

"Basically, that he'd asked himself the same question about the meaning of life after his wife died. It sounded as though he went through the same stages I've been going through—shock, anger...confusion. His letter was really beautiful."

Clint stared up at the stoplight, his fingers tightening on the steering wheel. He knew the knot in his stomach was ridiculous. He should be glad she'd found someone else who understood what she was going through. He wanted her to find someone, didn't he? She'd mourned John's death long enough. It was time for her to get on with her life—time for him to get on with his.

"You think this guy is sincere?" he asked tightly.

"Sincere? Yes." The idea that the letter writer might not be sincere seemed to surprise her. "Why wouldn't he be sincere?"

"He knows you're a widow. Maybe he's just trying to play on your emotions."

"Clint, you are a cynic."

He knew he was. He also knew she was too trusting. "Not everyone is as honest as John was. You don't even know if these men are actually writing these letters. Maybe they're getting someone else to write them."

"Why would they do that?"

"Because they want you to go out with them," he said, knowing Gary's motives.

"Well, I'm not interested in a date," she said firmly. "Not yet, at least. What about you, Clint?"

"Me?" He tensed, afraid to glance her way. Had she guessed his feelings for her? Did she know how often she filled his dreams?

She leaned forward, closing the space between the front seat and back, and he caught a whiff of her perfume, the scent teasingly seductive. "Are you honest?" she asked.

Honest. He knew he wasn't. He hadn't been honest with her from the day they'd met. "I've been known to tell a white lie or two."

"Such as?"

Such as telling her he was a chauffeur, nothing more. The light turned green, and he stepped on the accelerator, sending the Jag forward. "Such as telling my mother she's not getting any older looking."

The acceleration pushed Shannon back into the seat. That he'd even mentioned his mother was unusual for him. In the three years she'd known him, he'd said very little about his family. "Is your mother a widow?"

"Yes."

"How old were you when your father died?"

"Fourteen."

At least Clint had had his father for fourteen years. Hers had taken off when she was only three. After that, her mother had had "friends." Not that she blamed her mother for being cautious about another relationship, but the one thing Shannon had always wanted was a father. "Were you close to your father?"

Clint didn't answer, and after a minute or so she began to wonder if he'd heard her. She was about to repeat the question when he said, "There was a time when I wanted to be just like him."

His words were tense, and the fact that he didn't continue made her all the more curious. "But?"

He kept his gaze on the traffic ahead, and once again didn't answer for so long, she wondered if he was going to respond at all. Finally he spoke. "My father was killed in the process of robbing a liquor store, Shannon. I was there, too, along with my two older brothers. Both my father and older brother were killed. Clay and I got away."

"Oh." She'd known his past wasn't perfect, but she hadn't suspected he'd robbed stores, or that his father and brother had been killed in the process. "Were you ever caught?"

"No. I lucked out. I lucked out on a lot of things. My brother, Clay, however, is in Jackson State Prison for armed robbery. A different robbery. He did turn out just like our father." Clint glanced at her through the rearview mirror. "Makes you wonder about me, doesn't it? Wonder if those paintings and your jewelry are all that safe?"

There was a time she would have said yes. Not now. "I know you wouldn't rob me. You wouldn't rob anyone."

"You're sure?"

"I'm sure," she said firmly. Whatever he'd been, he wasn't that now. "What about your sister?"

"Lizzy." Clint paused, and Shannon could see his shoulders relax. "Now, there's a different story. She's the one good apple in the bunch."

"And you see yourself as a rotten apple?"

Again he glanced at her through the rearview mirror. "I've got a few blemishes. A lot of people would say I could go bad at any time."

"A lot of people don't know you," she said, wondering if she did. "You may be domineering, overbearing, stubborn and—"

"Me stubborn?" he interrupted. "You're the one who's insisting on writing to complete strangers, no matter what the possible consequences might be."

"The only possible consequences I see," she said, "is I might find these men interesting enough to want to meet them."

"Exactly."

Shannon wondered if Clarissa might be right, if Clint was resisting the idea because he was jealous. "Does that bother you?" she challenged. "Is it the idea of me getting together with another man that you're against?"

"Of course not," he insisted. "You should get together with other men. Date, get married...have children. It's just that you have to be careful."

"Meaning I have to pick someone suitable?" She'd heard it before. "Someone like you?"

He didn't hesitate. "Don't be silly. The type of men you should be meeting are the ones you'll meet here." He turned onto the drive to the country club, waved at the guard and drove on. "Here's where you should be looking."

"You make this place sound like hunting grounds."

"Here's where you'll find the men with money. Well-educated men. Businessmen."

Shannon glanced around at the well-manicured grounds, the expensive cars parked in the lot and the stately building ahead of them. John had loved coming here. She'd never felt completely comfortable. "Men who spend most of their time talking about money, golf or tennis. I sometimes wonder if they have any idea how most people live. You know, most of the members here think I married John for his money."

"They're wrong," Clint said without hesitation.

"They're wrong, but you know what's strange? When I was a kid, I always dreamed about having money...what it would be like. Now that I have it, I've discovered money is a burden."

"A lot of people would like to share that burden...or maybe, I should say, ease you of that burden." He brought the car to a stop and looked back at her. "If you had known what your life would be like, would you have thought twice about marrying John?"

"I did think twice," she said. "I was just seventeen. I wasn't sure I wanted to get married, wasn't sure I wasn't just looking for a father figure."

"But in the end—?"

"The decision was easy." She smiled. "I loved him. And that's how it will be if I marry again.... For love."

"She's a dreamer," Clint complained to Paul Green a month later. "A dreamer looking for love."

Paul looked up from the financial statement he'd been going over. "She's doing a good job managing the money she's inherited."

"I mean an emotional dreamer," Clint said. "She's still writing to those three men." And Clint was still helping Gary write back.

Gary might be copying the words in his own handwriting and might be signing his name, but Clint knew those were his own thoughts and feelings in the letters. And when he asked Shannon what her suitors had written lately, it pleased him when she quoted his words— after she'd sputtered that they weren't her suitors.

Not that he let on that he was pleased. "She's asking for trouble," he grumbled. "That's what she's doing."

"As long as she's simply writing to these men, what's the problem?"

"The problem is, in her last letter she suggested getting together for a coffee or something."

Paul cocked his head. "How do you know that?"

Clint immediately realized what he'd said. "I saw one of the letters . . . before she mailed it."

"Hmm." Paul's look was questioning. "And what do you plan on doing about this? She is a grown woman, after all. Having coffee with a man, well—"

"Is perfectly natural," Clint agreed. He sighed in frustration and began pacing the length of the den. Paul was the only one in the household who knew why Clint had been hired.

"Maybe it's time to tell her those guys rear-ended her car on purpose," Paul said. "If she knew she didn't pass out that day, that she would have been kidnapped if that police officer hadn't come along, maybe—?"

Clint shook his head. "I've thought about telling her the truth, almost have more than once, then I stop myself." He ceased his pacing and faced Paul. "John didn't want to tell her because he was afraid it would scare her. I'm afraid to tell her because I don't think it will matter to her, and once she knows why I was hired, I'll be out the door. Then who will watch over her? She's too damned trusting, Paul. In that way she's still like a child."

"She *was* a child when John married her. She's grown up a lot, especially this past year."

"Yes, she has, but she still doesn't realize people would kill to have the money she has."

"Because she sees the good in people."

"But as you and I know, not everyone is good."

Paul removed his glasses and rubbed the bridge of his nose, then looked back at Clint. "You ever thought of marrying her?"

"Me?"

"You." Paul nodded and slipped his glasses back into place. "You two have similar backgrounds."

Clint shook his head. "We're as different as night and day. She may have been raised in a poor neighborhood, but it was paradise compared to mine. No, there's nothing similar between us. She's a lady, and I'm a..." He shook his head again. He didn't know what he was, other than frustrated.

"I don't know," Paul said with a grin. "You two—"

Clint cut him off. "Are employer and employee, and I would quit this job in a minute if I didn't think I'd be letting John down. I've got a business to get started. This charade was only supposed to be for a couple of years. I didn't sign on for a lifetime."

Paul continued studying him, his pen pressed against his lips, and Clint wasn't sure he'd convinced him that he wasn't interested. He didn't need Paul guessing how he felt.

Finally Paul nodded. "So what do you plan on doing?"

"I'd like to get her interested in one of the guys at the country club, but since she seems intent on meeting these guys she's writing to, I guess it's time to call in a favor from an old Marine buddy who just happens to be working for the FBI."

3

"Why did you pick this Gary to meet first?" Clint asked Shannon as he held the door open to the Mercedes. "Why not one of the others?"

"I like Gary's letters best, what he has to say and how he says it." She slid into the back seat and looked up at him. "I know you don't approve, that you think all this is crazy and dangerous, but all I'm doing this evening is having a cup of coffee with a man. And you..." She smiled teasingly. "Will be right there."

Indeed he would be, Clint thought as he closed her door and got in behind the steering wheel. He wouldn't miss this for anything.

Last Monday, when Gary had walked into The Grill, the man had strutted up to Clint's table like a cocky rooster, had smugly slapped Shannon's letter down on the table and had gloated all evening. To hear him talk, he'd managed the feat on his own, and this coffee date was just a formality. Next stop, the Renaissance Center.

Clint had his doubts about that. As unpredictable as Shannon had been lately, he didn't think she'd lost all of her senses. Not wanting to date the upper crust of society was one thing. Falling for a social reject was another.

"The Poet's Café?" he asked, though she'd told him the name of the coffeehouse earlier that evening and Gary had mentioned it Monday.

"Over on Mack Avenue."

Clint started the car and pushed the button that swung open the gates blocking the drive. Another click once they were through and the gates swung closed. Few homes in Grosse Pointe were as well fortified as the Powell estate. Few homes took up a city block and housed a collection of original works of art that would make any museum director drool.

The remote-controlled gates were just one of the devices Clint had helped John Powell install. Clint had used what he'd learned on the streets, while in the Marines and while in college to plug the vulnerable spots in the estate's security. Gary's computer advice had filled in the remaining gaps.

Shannon knew of most of the devices that Clint had recommended, but not all. She didn't know how truly special her necklace from John was. The tracking device was smaller than a pea and gilded gold. It looked no different from the other pea-size balls of gold strung together.

John had asked her to wear the necklace at all times, and she had. She still wore it all the time, which gave Clint some measure of peace, considering how independent she was becoming.

"Gary's a computer programmer," Shannon said from the back seat. "He works at Braxton's, is thirty-five, has never been married and graduated from Oakland University."

"Thirty-five and never been married? Doesn't that make you wonder?" Clint glanced up at the rearview mirror to catch her reaction. He wasn't above planting a few seeds of doubt in her mind.

She seemed to take pause, but only for a second. "You're what? Thirty-three? Thirty-four?"

"Thirty-two," he admitted.

"And have you ever been married?"

He hesitated, then answered. "Yes."

Clint didn't think she knew that, and the surprise in her voice confirmed his guess. "Really? John told me you weren't married."

"I'm not. Not now."

Shannon laughed. "What happened? She get tired of you bossing her around?

"No." He hadn't expected the conversation to get this personal and wished he'd never brought up the subject of Gary's bachelorhood. Instead of pointing out the fact that there might be something wrong with a man who was thirty-five and unmarried, his comment had taken them to his past.

"So? Come on, Dawson," she persisted. "What happened?"

What had happened was he'd lost the one breath of sunshine that had stepped into his chaotic life. "My wife was killed in an auto accident."

"Oh..." The silence that filled the car was oppressive, then he heard her sigh. "I'm sorry."

He had been, too. Tanya's death had nearly undone all that he'd worked to achieve.

"I remember," Shannon said softly, "after John died, you said you understood what I was going through. You should have told me."

"It's not something I like to talk about." Not then, not now.

"Sometimes talking about it helps."

"Not for me." It simply made him angry. "I will say, you handled John's death a lot better than I did Tanya's."

"That was her name?"

"Yes." It had been a long time since he'd said it aloud. "Tanya Marie."

"You met her...?"

Shannon left the question unfinished. She was getting him to talk, making him remember. And, as usual, for her, he would. "I met her in the emergency room," he said. "She was a nurse. My bike and I had had a temporary parting of the ways, and I'd kissed the dirt. If you think I've got an ugly mug now, you should have seen my face that night."

"I don't think you have an 'ugly mug.'"

Shannon said it firmly, and he almost believed her. "I suppose you're going to tell me you haven't noticed my nose."

"It's a little crooked."

He laughed. "A little? Honey, I think you need your eyes checked."

"You're not bad looking," she insisted. "I'll bet your wife thought you were good-looking."

"She always was a little crazy." Helping him through college. Accepting his family. Loving him.

"How long were you married?"

"Two years." Two short years. "A drunk ran his car into hers. He walked away with minor injuries. They said she died instantly."

Clint shook his head, remembering his shock when the police officer came to his door and gave him the news. "I was like you when they told you about John. I wouldn't believe it at first... wouldn't accept it."

"With someone who's old or sick," she said, "you have time to prepare yourself. When someone goes out to play golf, looking as healthy as ever..."

Shannon didn't finish, but he understood. "It rocks you to the core."

"How many tears did I cry that first month?"

"A lot."

"I remember that night I started throwing things, and you came upstairs and stopped me. I didn't mean to hit you, I hope you know that. I was just so angry. At John for dying and leaving me, at the unfairness of it all."

"I understood." He'd heard the crash and had dashed up the stairs, afraid of what he might find. She'd been about to throw a lamp when he'd grabbed her. He'd wanted to take away her pain, to make it easier for her than it had been for him. "For six months after Tanya died, I drank a lot and got into fights."

"I guess, on some level, I knew you knew what I was going through. You helped me a lot."

"It was payback time. A friend of mine believes that everything that happens to us is a learning tool, and we must share what we learn."

"And what did you learn?"

"That words don't help, only time does. You think you'll never love again, but it can happen. Does happen."

"Has it happened for you, Clint? Have you found someone else to love?"

He realized what he'd said, and silently chastised himself. Lately he was blabbering like a stool pigeon to Shannon. Next thing he knew, he'd be telling her everything.

He kept his answer ambiguous. "Maybe."

Shannon knew Clint's personal life was none of her business, but Clarissa's suggestion that he might see her as more than just an employer and friend had been playing in the back of her mind ever since that conversation. In the weeks since, she'd tried to see something in the way Clint looked at her, spoke to her or acted. She hadn't. He was his usual self, driving her wherever she needed to go, there when she needed him, but always slightly aloof. Only by prodding did she get him to talk. So she prodded. "'Maybe,' like a yes or a no?"

"That café's the next block or two, isn't it?" he asked, and Shannon knew all the prodding in the world wasn't going to help this time. He wasn't going to answer her question.

"We're close," she confirmed, remembering the one time she had been there with one of the women from the country club. The place had just opened at the time.

"I hope you know what you're doing," he said. "This idea of meeting men you don't know—"

Another lecture was coming. "Clint, I'm just having coffee with the guy. His letters fascinate me. Some of the things he says are exactly what I've been thinking. It's like we're on the same wavelength."

"Like that comment of his about the bumps making you appreciate the smooth?" Clint asked.

She shouldn't have read that to him. "Okay, so sometimes what he says is a little corny." It was the rest of the letter she'd enjoyed, the parts about interwoven destinies and the sweet sadness of memories of the past. "Why don't you like Gary?"

"How can I dislike him? I don't even know him."

"Exactly."

And neither did she, Shannon knew. She might be putting up a front for Clint, but the idea of having coffee with a computer programmer who could write such thought-provoking letters had kept her nervous all week. Would he be disappointed in her? Sure, she'd learned a lot in the years she'd been married to John, especially from their trips abroad, but she was still a college dropout from a poor Detroit neighborhood who hadn't even known Burgundy was a wine, much less an area in France.

She'd never felt comfortable around John's mother, when Madeline Powell was still alive, and she certainly didn't feel comfortable at the country club. "I'm going to sell my membership at the yacht club, and I'm thinking of selling my membership at the country club," she said. Not that Clint needed to know, although selling her membership for the country club would eliminate three trips a week. No more bridge games. No more golf.

"Why?"

"John is the one who loved the yacht. How many times have I gone out?"

"Why sell your membership at the country club?"

The answer was simple. "I don't feel like I belong."

"Of course you belong. You have every right to be there."

She saw him glance up at the rearview mirror and knew he was looking at her, watching her reaction. Clint always treated her as though she'd grown up with a silver spoon in her mouth. So had John.

"Let me rephrase that," she said. "I don't *want* to belong. Spending my afternoons playing cards seems such a waste of time, and I've never been that wild about the game of golf. Sure, it's all right, but—"

"The country club is a good place for you to meet the right type of men."

"So you keep telling me, but I met John when I was working at Mabel's Diner." He'd had car trouble, had come in to use the telephone, had a coffee while he waited for the tow service and they'd talked. For the next two weeks he stopped by every night she was working. Four weeks after that, they were married.

"A chance occurrence, from what he told me."

"Or fate?" She would never know. "Clint, I'm not looking to meet men."

"Aren't you?" he asked, and she realized the irony of what she'd said. She was on her way to meet a man.

"I'm meeting with Gary because his letters fascinate me. There's the coffeehouse."

The Poet's Café was on the right-hand corner of the block, and Clint slowed the car as they drove past. There was a sectioned-off area to the side for those who wanted to be outside. She glanced over the handful of people seated at those tables. One of the three men could be Gary. In his letters, he'd said he was average height, had brown hair and hazel eyes. He'd also admitted that he wore glasses, but only for reading. That eliminated the short balding man with the thick glasses seated by himself, but one of the two men seated at another table would fit the description.

Butterflies invaded her stomach, churning away, and she was tempted to tell Clint to simply turn around and head back to the house. What was she doing, anyway? Clint was right, though she would never admit it to him. Meeting a man she'd merely written to was crazy.

"There's a spot," he said and pulled into a parking space.

Shannon took in a deep breath. It was too late to turn back.

Clint parked the car and held the door for her. He was surprised when she didn't question his going with her. He'd expected an argument. It was getting so he didn't know what to expect next from her.

Walking a few steps back, he followed her toward the coffee house. He hadn't seen Gary yet, and two of the men seated at the tables outside were eyeing Shannon with more than just a passing glance. Not that he blamed them.

She'd left her hair down, so it flowed loosely over her shoulders like a silken wave, and the flowery dress she was wearing enhanced her feminine curves, its short length showing off her legs. He'd been having a rough time not reacting ever since she'd walked down the stairs. He could imagine the effect she was having on the other men. The darker-haired of the two at the table smiled enticingly, and she started toward him.

Clint wasn't sure what to do. To say anything would clue her in that he knew what Gary looked like. To say nothing meant hoping she'd realize the mistake before it went too far.

Gary solved the problem.

Out of the café he came, wobbling slightly. He looked different than usual, and Clint understood why. Gary Cleveland was wearing no glasses and had a full head of hair. A thick, dark brown, unnaturally full head of hair.

He bumped into a table where two women sat, one nursing a glass of soda, another a cup of coffee. Apologizing to the women, he squinted at Shannon. She was headed straight for him, but her gaze was still on the man seated at the table just to Gary's side. Gary waved, grinning like a jack-o'-lantern, then called out her name.

She stopped and looked his way. Clint could tell she wasn't sure what to make of Gary. That was when three teenage boys came out of the café, one walking backward and talking to his friends. The boy wasn't aware that Gary had stopped next to the table, and like a scene in a slapstick comedy movie, he bumped into Gary, knocking him off balance. Struggling for stability, Gary grabbed the edge of the table.

The table didn't hold him.

Though the two women tried to stop it, the table and Gary went down, and the soda glass and coffee cup crashed on the cement flooring, splashing soda and coffee far and wide. Shannon jumped back, but not far enough or soon enough. Syrup-sweetened soda spattered over her bare legs and up the front of her dress.

"Oh, damn . . . I, oh . . ." Gary scrambled to his feet, trying to right the table and apologize to the women and Shannon at the same time. "I didn't want our first meeting to be like this."

She stared at him. "You're Gary?"

Shannon glanced over at the dark-haired man at the other table, then back at Gary, and Clint knew which of the two men she would have preferred. Women could say what they liked about a man's looks not being important, but they always migrated to the handsome ones.

"At your service," Gary said and dropped back down to his knees in front of her. Immediately he began dabbing at her legs with a napkin. The built-up heels on Gary's shoes were quite obvious.

Shannon noticed them, but she was too stunned to comprehend. Here they hadn't even formally met, and the man was on his knees, fondling her legs. It wasn't exactly the greeting she'd envisioned.

She stared down at the top of his head. The color of his hair was so dark. The texture so—

His hand began to inch up under her skirt, and she pulled back. "What do you think you are doing?"

"I . . ." He scrambled to his feet, his expression childlike. "I only—"

"Never mind. Forget it," she said. She certainly would like to forget it.

The pudgy man in front of her didn't fit any of her expectations. Her letter writer had had a flair with words, an eloquence of thought. She'd pictured someone taller, someone self-assured and poised, not a munchkin in an ill-fitting, wrinkled suit, who might not be wearing glasses, but from the way he was squinting and groping about, should be.

"You, ah..." He looked inside the coffeehouse. "You want something to drink? A coffee or a soda?"

What she wanted was to get out of there, to pretend she didn't know the man. And she might have done just that, if she hadn't noticed Clint standing to the side, smiling smugly. She could practically hear him saying, "I told you so."

"A coffee sounds good," she said, smiling at Gary. Brazenly she slid her arm through his.

The Poet's Café was only moderately busy, and there were several empty tables. He guided her to one, helping her with her chair. She noticed Clint come in, too. He hung back by the door.

"Cappuccino? Latte? Or...?" Gary asked, grinning.

"Just plain coffee." Her stomach wasn't up to anything rich or fancy. "Decaf."

"Decaf it is."

Gary headed for the counter, his steps slightly wobbly, and she knew he wasn't used to walking on elevated heels. If he had been, she was sure he wouldn't have walked so close to the plant hanging by the counter.

It was succulent, thick and heavy, hanging over the edge of the pot like a moose's rack. As Gary walked by, one branch barely touched the top of his head. He walked on.

His hair stayed.

She bit her lower lip to keep from laughing. The top of Gary's head now showed a balding spot. Clint walked over to where the toupee hung from the plant. He looked her way, smiled, then disentangled the hair.

She watched Clint get in line behind Gary. Clint said something, and Gary reached up and touched the bare spot on his head. Quickly he took the toupee and put it back on his head. His face ruddy, Gary didn't look her way, not until he started back to the table with two mugs of coffee.

Shannon said nothing about the incident. She was afraid if she did, she'd start laughing. She definitely didn't look at Clint.

"Here you are," Gary said, setting one mug in front of her, then sitting himself on the opposite side of the table.

She took one quick look at his hair, noticed it wasn't on straight, and decided to concentrate on his eyes. "The eyes are the windows of the soul," she said aloud. He was a man who liked clichés. At least, he'd used several in his letters, and it might start a conversation.

He frowned. "What's wrong with my eyes?"

"Nothing. I was just . . ." She shrugged. "Nothing."

"I only need my glasses for reading, and working on the computer. I can see well enough. That's not why I fell outside. It was that kid."

"I know." She wished he'd just forget it. "So finally we meet. The written word can become the spoken word."

"Yeah . . . right."

He reached for his mug of coffee, but she could tell he'd misjudged the distance and was going to put his fingers into the coffee. "Gary . . . ?" she started, but not soon enough.

He gave a squeal that could be heard through the small shop, then stuck his fingers into his mouth. "Just testing if it was hot," he said, a muscle in his cheek twitching.

"I take it it's hot," she said, forcing herself not to laugh.

"Not bad," he said, and again reached for the mug, this time slowly.

He found the handle without a problem, and she tried to convince herself that everything that was happening was simply because he was nervous. "I've really enjoyed your letters. They've made me think."

"The letters. Yeah . . . right." He glanced around the room, then grinned at her. "Now you can get to know the real me."

"I'm glad."

He sat back, taking on a confident, jaunty air. "In one of your letters, you said you like people to be honest, to say exactly what they're thinking. To get to the point."

"That's right."

"With you, a man should say what he wants, right?"

"Right," she agreed, nodding.

"Well, what I want is to spend a weekend with you."

"To what?" She stared at him, certain she'd misunderstood.

"I won a weekend at the Renaissance Center." He grinned proudly. "We get champagne. Dinner in the room."

She laughed. "You've got to be kidding."

His grin disappeared. "No, I'm serious. It's all free."

"I don't even know you."

"Well . . ." He shrugged, his cheek twitching. "It doesn't have to be this weekend. We could do it—"

Shaking her head, she stopped him. "I'm not spending a weekend with you at some hotel."

"We're talking the Renaissance Center."

"I don't care where," she said, hoping she was making herself clear. "Look, I like honesty, but . . ." She couldn't believe he'd even asked. "You said it yourself in one of your letters, people need to get to know each other . . . need to know themselves."

"I know who I am," Gary said, grinning cockily. "And I know who you are."

"But I'm not sure I know who I am." And that bothered her. "I remember you writing that we each need to be true to ourselves, to decide what is of value and what to turn away from."

"Sure, but—"

She didn't let him finish. "What I didn't completely understand was the vision you mentioned."

"Vision?" He frowned. "What vision?"

"You wrote it in your last letter. You said we all need a vision."

"Oh, yeah, he said you'd like that," Gary said, then stopped and looked at her. "I mean, I knew you'd like that."

"*He* said I'd like it?" She'd heard exactly what Gary had said.

"I meant me."

Gary nervously glanced around the coffeehouse, avoiding eye contact, and she understood. "You didn't write those letters, did you?"

"Well, I..." His left cheek began to twitch badly. "It was my handwriting."

"But whose words, whose thoughts?" She wanted to know.

Gary looked beyond her, as though searching for help. Shannon glanced that way and understood Gary's concern. Clint had risen to his feet.

She smiled. Good ol' Clint to the rescue. Not that she wanted to be rescued just yet. First she wanted to know who'd written Gary's letters. "So what is his name? Who is the Cyrano de Bergerac behind those letters?"

"I only thought," Gary said, fumbling for his mug. "I mean he..." His gaze was riveted on Clint.

"Don't!" Clint demanded.

The mug of coffee dropped out of Gary's hand, hitting the table with a thud and splashing coffee into the air. Shannon pushed her chair back and stood. One dousing an evening was enough. Turning, she faced Clint. "We're leaving."

"But, Shannon," Gary whined. He'd stood and was wiping coffee from his suit.

She looked at him, certain one day she would laugh about this moment. Now, however, she only wanted to escape. "Tell Cyrano to write his own letters," she said, and walked away.

"Don't say a word," she warned Clint as she passed him. "Not one word."

Clint kept quiet, but he glared at Gary. One thing he didn't need was Shannon knowing he'd written those letters. He'd been an idiot to get involved, should have said no from the very start. He'd revealed too much of himself in those letters. Far too much.

Meekly Gary sank back into his chair, his expression defeated, and Clint followed Shannon out of the café.

"I can't believe that guy," she said from the back seat of the Mercedes. "What a creep."

Clint said nothing.

"Go ahead, say it!" she demanded.

"You told me not to. 'Not one word,' I quote."

"Right." He heard her disgruntled sigh, then she repeated, "What a creep. Everything you warned me about was true. You can't get to know someone through letters." Again she sighed. "No, that's not true, either. I think I was getting to know someone—it just wasn't Gary Cleveland."

She sat forward, her head coming close to his shoulder. "Can you believe him? He actually got someone else to write his letters. He didn't even know what I was talking about when I asked him what he meant by a vision."

Clint played ignorant. "Vision?"

"Well, I'd written that I really didn't know what I wanted to be when I grew up, and he wrote—or at least this other person wrote—that we all need a vision."

"Interesting. And what do *you* think he meant?"

"I don't know." She laughed. "But my vision isn't going to include one Gary Cleveland."

She sat back, and he allowed himself a smile. He'd known he had better taste than to be attracted to someone like Gary.

"Do you know the story of Cyrano de Bergerac?" she asked.

He not only knew it, he'd just played a part in it. "I've heard of it."

"I had to read it for an English class," she said. "It always seemed so sad to me. Here was this man, in love with his cousin Roxane, and all she wanted was this dumb pretty boy."

"If I recall, Cyrano did have one very, very big nose." The parallels were there.

"I'm going to have to rent the movie sometime."

"And?"

"Watch it. I liked the story."

"Liked the idea of a man pouring out his heart and losing in the end?"

"Roxane did realize in the end that Cyrano had written the letters, that he was the one she was in love with."

"He was a fool for wasting his time on her." Just as he was a fool.

"And you're a cynic." She sighed. "You shouldn't have yelled at him."

"Cyrano?"

"No, Gary. He might have told me who the guy was who wrote the letters."

That was what he'd been afraid Gary would do. "The way he was groping around, I thought he was going to spill that coffee."

She laughed. "What a klutz he was. Of course, you coming to my rescue didn't help the poor guy."

"I wasn't coming to your rescue."

"Yes, you were. You always do. You're always there to protect me."

"I was getting up to get a napkin," he said. "I'd forgotten one."

"Sure." She laughed. "When are you going to admit that John hired you to watch over me?"

Clint knew she was fishing, and he had to be careful how he phrased his answer. "If that were true, wouldn't I be by your side at all times? Would I have let you get soda all over your dress?"

"You weren't that far away. I have a feeling you're never that far away."

He said nothing, keeping his gaze on the street. The gates to the estate were less than a half mile away, and he was already checking the area for anything that might look different from the norm.

4

As usual, Shannon got nothing more from Clint, and she noticed, as soon as he had her safely ensconced in the house, he disappeared. To talk to Angelo, he said. She suspected his retreat was to avoid talking to her.

At ten o'clock, she went upstairs, showered and crawled into the king-size bed she'd once shared with John. She thought she'd go right to sleep, but the darkness triggered memories, her mind replaying the scene at the coffeehouse. From the moment Gary had identified himself, he'd been a disappointment. The hair had been a laugh, the elevated heels ridiculous and the only thing he'd proved by not wearing glasses was he couldn't see.

"What a phony," she muttered and rolled over.

Within seconds, she was remembering Gary's letters. His prose had enlightened, amused and flattered her; his words were simple yet poetic. Writing to him had been like writing to a friend.

"A phony friend," she grumbled and tried another position.

At eleven o'clock she opened the window, hoping the sounds from Lake Erie would lull her to sleep. At midnight, she gave up the effort. Since she'd been a child, there'd been one thing she'd taken when she couldn't get to sleep. From her earliest memories, it had been hot milk that had lulled her into dreamland.

She slipped on a robe but skipped the slippers. Barefooted, she left her bedroom, proceeded down the hall to the stairs and, as quietly as possible, descended. Clint's room was to the right of the front door. It had originally been a guest room, though when she and John were first married and John's mother was still alive and inhabiting the upstairs master bedroom, the downstairs bedroom had been theirs. It was spacious and had its own bathroom. A perfect place for Clint to live, John had insisted when he'd hired Clint, and she hadn't objected.

She knew now that John was gone, some tongues were wagging with the speculation of what might be going on in the big house between one twenty-seven-year-old widow and her chauffeur. Not that she cared what others said, and she certainly wasn't going to ask Clint to move into the bungalow by the garage with Clarissa and Angelo. They deserved their privacy, and so did he.

She tiptoed past Clint's room and into the kitchen. As quietly as she could, she closed the door. Only then did she snap on the light and head for the refrigerator.

She was facing the microwave, watching the timer count down the seconds before her milk would be hot enough to work its magic, when she heard the kitchen door being opened. Turning, she faced Clint and felt a lump the size of one of his fists form in her stomach.

He stood framed in the doorway, his dark hair mussed and a sleepy look in his dark eyes. He wore his gray slacks, but no socks or shoes, and no shirt or jacket. Bare-chested, he looked even more powerful and intimidating than ever. A warrior in his prime.

A man—virile and sexy.

She swallowed hard and found herself unable to draw her gaze from his brawny shoulders or the dark hairs that curled in a mat across his chest. In a wavy T, those hairs tapered down to the waistband of his slacks, then disappeared, leaving too much to her imagination. That his belt wasn't buckled but hung dangling open didn't help curtail the direction of her thoughts. Everything about the man was suggestive, and her body was responding to the suggestion. The swelling in her breasts and the heat generating between her legs spoke of a need she didn't want to acknowledge.

It had been over a year since she'd slept with a man. All that time, Clint had been around, but not once, no matter what others might say, had she thought about going to bed with him.

She was thinking about it now.

The chime of the timer went off, and she jumped, the knot in her stomach growing tighter. Turning away from Clint, she faced the microwave, arousal turning to anger. "What are you doing, spying on me?"

"I heard a sound," he said calmly.

"I wanted some hot milk. Go back to bed."

She knew she sounded like a grouch. He made her feel grouchy. Edgy. Unnerved. Taking the mug of milk from the microwave, she faced the doorway again, hoping he'd left.

He stood there, staring at her.

"What?" she demanded, lifting her chin and cradling the mug in her hands.

"Do you need anything?" he asked.

Yes, I need something, she silently screamed and stared at him, marveling at how beautifully his body was put together, each muscle so well-defined. She could imagine him totally naked, nothing covering his masculinity, and she could imagine him making love with her.

Deep inside, the desire grew stronger, and she felt her legs tremble. Quickly she headed for one of the stools by the counter.

"No, I don't need anything," she lied, her voice shaky. "I couldn't sleep, that's all. I thought a little hot milk would help."

"Good idea."

Seated, she stared at her mug, watching the steam rise from the milk and hoping Clint would go away—wishing the heat within her would go away. The sound of his bare feet on the kitchen linoleum warned her that he was coming closer. Tensed, she watched him go to the sink and reach for a glass. The ripple of his back muscles didn't help the rippling sensation between her legs. She squeezed her thighs together, and took a sip of the hot milk, but her gaze never left his back.

Clint stared out the window over the sink. His body blocked Shannon's reflection, but he knew she was watching him. From the moment he'd stepped into the kitchen, he'd known he'd made a mistake. The look in her eyes was different tonight. Intense.

Hungry.

Deep inside, a hunger gnawed at him.

He should go back to bed. Should get the hell out of the kitchen. Though he'd seen her in a robe and nightgown before, tonight was different. Tonight he wanted to remove that robe and nightgown, remove his own clothing and press her body against his. Tonight he wanted to make love with her, claim her as his and—

The water ran over the edge of glass onto his hand, shocking him back to reality. He turned off the tap, and faced her. She wasn't his and never would be, and he had no right to think of making love with her. She'd moved beyond him, to a better life. What he needed was a kick in the pants.

"Don't let tonight discourage you," he said, determined to get his thoughts on the right track. "So the guy got someone else to write his letters. After meeting him, are you surprised? He couldn't even walk up to you without making a scene, much less talk to you. But that doesn't mean your other letter writers aren't writing their own letters or will be as bad. Give them a chance."

For a moment she stared at him, a slight frown creasing the smooth line of her forehead; then slowly a grin formed, the smile reaching her eyes and giving them the brilliance he loved. "Am I hearing this right?" she asked. "You, Clint Dawson, are encouraging me to continue writing these letters? Are telling me to go out with these guys?"

"At least meet them." He'd checked out both men. Martin P. Harwick, Ph.D. was a full professor, thirty-eight years old and had had two papers published on Lord Byron. Though what he earned teaching at the University of Michigan was a pittance compared to the money Shannon had inherited, he was intelligent, well traveled and would make her a good husband.

Edward J. Sitwell had been hired as the CEO of the Southerly Company in Dearborn three years ago and in that time had doubled the company's earnings. A widower for five years, he did have two preteenage children that might complicate matters, but he was Clint's pick for Shannon. In many ways, he wasn't all that different from John Powell, simply closer to Shannon's age and less wealthy.

Once again she frowned. "Okay, what's up? Why this change of heart?"

"No change of heart. If writing to these men has given you pleasure, perhaps you should meet them."

"And face another fiasco like tonight's?"

"I don't see how all three could be that bad."

"Let's hope not." Slowly a smile curved her lips. "When you picked that toupee off that branch and gave it to him, I thought I was going to burst out laughing. And those heels. I don't think I was that bad when I wore my first heels. Why can't people just be honest about who they are and what they want?"

"For some, it's too scary." Honesty meant telling the truth and taking the consequences.

"That was one thing about John," she said with a sigh. "He may not have talked a lot, but what he said was the truth."

At least, in part the truth, Clint knew. He, too, had admired John's honesty and integrity. That the man had loved his wife so much, he was willing to lie for her sake was something Clint could understand.

"Ever wonder what your destiny is, Clint?" Shannon asked.

"My destiny?"

She'd asked that question in her last letter to Gary, and what he'd written back for Gary was basically the Clint Dawson philosophy on destiny. To give her the same answer now would certainly clue her in on his part of Gary's sham.

"Destiny?" he repeated once again, then shrugged. "I guess what happens happens."

Shannon looked down at her milk. She'd hoped for more from him, for something deeper or at least more thought provoking. His body was turning her on; she wanted his mind to do the same.

She, evidently, wanted too much.

"Gary, in his last letter—or at least the person who was writing those letters for him—said he thought we made our own destiny, that our personalities and families play a part in that destiny, but we constantly make choices that can carry us above or beyond our DNA structures or environment."

"And do you agree?"

He didn't sound as though he did. "I'm not sure. I know certain choices I've made have taken me in different directions from my friends."

"Like marrying John?"

He smiled, and she liked how it changed his face. Earlier that evening, he'd referred to his face as an ugly mug. She saw it as intriguing, rugged and telling. His was a face that spoke of a rough life, a life that might have destroyed a weaker man but had made him stronger. His was also a face that mirrored a sensitivity that came from seeing too much despair. Growing up, she'd seen that kind of despair. "Marrying John certainly did change my life."

"You still miss him, don't you?"

Once again she looked down at her mug of milk. She wasn't sure if Clint would understand. She wasn't sure she understood. "I miss him, but what's really weird is it all seems like a dream. How we met, our marriage. The trips. Everything." She sighed and looked up at Clint. "I loved him. I really did. But now—"

"It's been almost a year and a half since he died," Clint reminded her. "You've cried your tears and mourned your loss. Now it's time to move on."

"I feel so guilty."

"You shouldn't. John wouldn't want you mourning him for the rest of your life. He wanted you happy."

"I'm not exactly unhappy, I'm just—" She wasn't sure she could explain.

"Restless?"

She shrugged. *Restless* wasn't exactly right, either. "I don't know what I want to be when I grow up. I have all this money, but—"

"No goals."

"No goals. No destiny." She half laughed. "Which brings us back to those letters I thought Gary was writing. The reason I wanted to meet him was I felt he understood. Those letters were everything I wanted and needed—the sweet, romantic words and the thought-provoking questions. Writing to him was making me think about what I do want to do with the rest of my life. It was like talking to a friend, a nonjudgmental friend who let me ramble on and didn't criticize."

"You don't feel that way with the other two you're writing to?"

"No. At least not yet. Maybe it will come."

"Maybe if you meet them."

"You're really pushing this, aren't you?" Grinning, she stood and walked over to where he stood by the sink. His change of attitude had her curious. "Why?"

She heard him suck in a breath and saw his chest expand. Reaching out, she touched the hairs on his body, feeling their coarse thickness and the warmth of him.

The moment she did, she knew she shouldn't have.

For a while she'd been able to ignore the chemistry between them; for a while she'd again seen him as a friend, nothing more. One touch had changed that. Slowly she let her gaze travel from his chest to his face.

"I . . ." he started, his voice husky. Quickly he cleared his throat. "If you meet them, you'll know if they're what you're looking for."

She could feel the tension within him. Tension radiated through her. Never looking away from his eyes, she teasingly let her hand move to the center of his chest.

The rapid beat of his heart pulsed through her palm, his skin hot, almost as hot as hers. Softly she said, "The problem is, I'm not sure what I'm looking for."

He swallowed hard. "It...it didn't take you long to make up your mind about Gary."

"No it didn't." She'd never heard him stammer before, not like this, and the hoarseness in his voice was seductive, the musky, male scent of his body teasing her senses.

She stepped even closer.

"I..."

His heart was beating a staccato against her palm, the rise and fall of his chest rapid. He put his hands on her shoulders, his gaze locked with hers, and she was sure he was going to pull her even closer.

She wasn't prepared when he set her back a step and eased himself to the side. "I'll see you in the morning," he said firmly and started for the door.

Stunned, Shannon watched him walk away. Her body ached for his touch, the need deep within her yearning for satisfaction. She knew she'd excited him, that for a moment he'd seen her as a woman, not an employer. For a moment he'd wanted her.

But only for a moment.

Anger was her first reaction. She turned toward the sink, and slammed her fist on the counter. Eyes closed, she didn't look to see if Clint stopped or glanced back. He'd rejected her. Had walked away from her. He'd...

She took in a deep breath, the realization of what she'd done seeping through her with startling clarity. She'd tried to seduce him, had thrown herself at him.

She heard the click of the kitchen door and knew he was gone. Slowly she opened her eyes, the window over the sink reflecting the emptiness of the room. A heaviness filled her.

How could she face him the next morning?

Dumping the rest of her milk in the sink, she placed Clint's glass and her mug in the dishwasher, snapped off the kitchen light and started for her room. She paused outside his door. She could apologize. Probably should.

Shannon stepped to his door, lifted her hand to knock, then hesitated. What would she say? Sorry, but I had the temporary hots for you, it won't happen again? Wear more clothes if you don't want me mauling you?

What she needed to do was go to bed—alone. She needed to get her head on straight. Turning away, she walked up the stairs.

Clint stood on the other side of the door. He'd heard her come near and had held his breath, not sure if he wanted her to knock and force him to talk to her or if he wanted her to go away. In the kitchen he'd nearly given in. It had taken all of his willpower to resist the temptation to take her into his arms.

Knowing what he should and should not do was one thing; resisting her touch was another. In her eyes he'd seen the need, and he'd wanted to nuzzle her neck, to inhale the provocative scent of her perfume and nibble at her soft flesh. He'd wanted to cup her breasts in his hands, to bare them to his sight and take them into his mouth. It would have been so easy to discover all of her secrets, to touch and caress her until she cried for fulfillment.

It would have been so easy to have made love to her.

He closed his eyes, banishing the thought. He could not make love with her, not tonight or any night. Going into the kitchen without more clothing on had been a mistake on his part. He'd known she was no intruder, no threat to the security of the house. He'd known she was upset with the events of the evening.

He should have realized the danger.

He'd been in bed when he'd heard her come down the stairs. He hadn't been able to sleep. Gary's show at the coffeehouse had been exactly what Clint had expected. It was a shame in a way that the guy tried so hard. He had a lot to offer, if he'd just accept who he was instead of trying to be someone else.

That was what Clint had been trying to convey to Shannon in the letters he'd written for Gary. That she'd liked his letters pleased him. That he would no longer be writing to her left an emptiness he hadn't expected. As much as he'd complained about each letter Gary had coerced him to write, while writing to her he'd felt connected to her. In those letters he'd been able to say the things he couldn't say to her face.

Going to his desk, he opened the drawer that held the gray paper he'd used for the drafts that Gary had later copied. He knew Gary had added a bit here and there. His "personal touch," Gary had said. Clint also knew Gary hadn't added much.

"Tell Cyrano to write his own letters," Shannon had said to Gary. Clint stared at the gray paper.

Should he? Did he dare?

Sitting down at his desk, he pulled out a sheet of the paper and grabbed a pen.

Shannon dreaded seeing Clint the next morning. She didn't eat much of her cereal. She couldn't. There was a rock of embarrassment in her stomach.

Long into the night, she'd tried to come up with the right words to erase what she had done. None had come. All she could say was she was sorry and it wouldn't happen again.

He came into the dining room as Clarissa refilled her coffee. "Morning," he said, nodding formally. "What is on the agenda today?"

"I may go up to the club for lunch." She waited for Clarissa to leave the room. As soon as the woman stepped into the kitchen, Shannon lowered her voice. "Clint, about last night—"

"Quite an experience," he said, not letting her finish. "Being around that Gary guy for a while could make a person do all sorts of crazy things."

He was making her excuses for her, giving her an out. She decided to take it. "Definitely quite an experience."

"You'll want the car around eleven-thirty?"

She nodded. "Eleven-thirty would be fine."

Two weeks later, Shannon stood in her office, staring at the envelope in her hand. Afraid her behavior with Clint had been triggered from sexual frustration, she'd accepted two dates during that time. She'd attended the ABA Gold Cup Thunderfest hydroplane races with Mitch from the club and the ITT Automotive Detroit Grand Prix with Brendon, who was a doctor at the hospital where she volunteered. As dates went, they'd been okay. There were no repeats of her fiasco with Gary. As releases for any sexual frustrations, she felt they'd failed.

Both men had kissed her, and she was sure either would have gone to bed with her if she'd been willing. That was the problem. Whatever crazy hormones had triggered her behavior the night in her kitchen, they weren't there with Mitch or Brendon. One kiss each was enough for her. The next time they called she turned them down.

During those two weeks, she'd also received letters from Martin and Ed and had answered each. Though Clint had suggested she meet with each of them, as she had with Gary, she was almost afraid to. Her experience with Gary had ended with her no longer receiving letters from him. She didn't want to chance that happening with either Martin or Ed.

Cyrano.

The name was in the upper left corner of the envelope in her hand, a P.O. box number below. The post office wasn't located in the best area around Detroit, nor the worst.

He'd written.

She turned the envelope over, trying to decide if she should open it or not. Was this from the person who'd written those letters for Gary, or was it from Gary himself? She wouldn't put it past the guy. He'd had the gall to show up at her gate two days after that coffee date, whining and whimpering that he deserved another chance. At least that's how Angelo had described his behavior.

For once she'd been glad Clint sometimes acted like a bodyguard. She'd sent him out to talk to Gary. When he came back, Clint had said Gary wouldn't be bothering her anymore.

Had he been wrong? Was Gary now trying to get to her through a letter?

Shannon tore the envelope in half, and watched half a sheet of gray paper flutter to the floor. Stooping, she picked it up. The page looked as if it had been crumpled, then flattened out, and the handwriting was different from what she'd received before. No exaggerated curves or flourishes. This writing was tighter and more controlled. She read part of a line. "In the strangest of ways, we are linked." The sentence ended along the ragged edge of the wrinkled, torn paper.

She skipped to the next line. "...affect the ebb and flow of our—"

Curious, she pulled out the other half of the letter and let the two parts of the envelope fall to the floor. For a moment, she tried holding the two halves of wrinkled gray paper together; then she gave up and carried them over to her desk. She was taping the sheet back together when the sound of Clint's voice startled her.

"I was looking at the Mercedes—" he began.

Like a child caught in the cookie jar, she jerked her hand back from the letter, dropping the roll of tape. It fell to the floor with a dull thud and rolled toward Clint.

"I didn't mean to scare you," he said, stepping into the room and picking up the roll of tape. That he had startled her surprised him. She normally wasn't that jumpy.

Taking another step into the room, Clint picked up the two halves of the envelope that lay on the floor. Fitting them together, he glanced at the return address, then at her. "You got a letter from Cyrano?"

She shrugged. "He wrote."

"But—?" It was impossible . . . unless. "Can I see it?"

"No, you can't see it," she said, frowning and stepping protectively in front of her desk.

He held up the envelope halves. "You tore it in half."

"And now I'm taping it together." She didn't move from her position. "You were saying something about the Mercedes?"

"I, ah—I think you should get new shocks." He could see a part of the torn sheet of paper on her desk. It looked like the same paper he'd used. It also looked like the paper had been crumpled then straightened out. The last time he'd seen the letter was when he was at his mother's. He'd taken it there, still unsure if he should mail it or not. After reading it again, he'd made up his mind, had crumpled it into a ball and had dropped it into a wastebasket. Now it had resurfaced . . . if it was his letter. "What did this Cyrano say?"

"I don't know. I haven't read it yet. Something about an ebb and flow."

He didn't react, but he knew it was his letter. How she'd gotten it was the question.

Once again, he looked at the envelope parts, then smiled. He had a feeling his sister could tell him how a thrown-away letter could end up in Shannon's hands. The next time he saw Lizzy, they were going to have to have a little talk.

"The guy's probably some kind of a nut," he said, certain that was how Shannon was going to feel once she read what he'd written.

"Probably," she agreed and held out her hand. "May I have the tape?"

"Sure." He handed her the roll of tape.

"And the envelope?"

Reluctantly he handed the envelope parts to her, too. "It's a post office address, and not in a very upscale neighborhood."

"So I noticed."

"I wouldn't write back if I were you."

She smiled. "You wouldn't have written back to any of them if you'd been me."

"Look what happened with Gary."

"True, but if you'll recall, I asked for this letter. I told Gary to tell Cyrano to write his own letters. Now he has."

"Under a phony name."

She started to say something, then stopped herself. "If you think the Mercedes needs new shocks, then get new shocks. That's your department, Clint."

Her message was clear, and Clint knew she was right. What she did in her personal life shouldn't be the business of a chauffeur, and to say anything more would be to say too much. Straightening his shoulders, he nodded. "I'll take care of it this afternoon."

Shannon waited until he'd left the room before she finished taping the letter. Only then did she turn the page over. Leaning back against her desk, she began to read.

Roxane, Roxane,
I hide from your view, ashamed of what I am and ashamed of what I've done. To be a part of a lie is unforgivable; yet I am trapped in a web of lies, a foolish victim and a perpetrator in the same. Only on paper can I speak my true feelings.

I was there the night you met Gary. I watched the farce. Watched you grow angry, and felt the lash of your tongue. I give no excuses, and should you decide to shred this letter into a thousand tiny pieces, I will understand. All I can say is writing to you has been my sustenance, the wine of my happiness. Four times I was able to speak what was in my heart. Four times I hoped the answers I gave helped light your way. Though you don't know who I am, I know you.

I have seen the warmth of your smiles, heard the joy in your laughter. I have suffered through your sadness, and each day it lessens, I find delight. I am the shadows that lurk in the past, and you are the sunlight of the future. As you grow stronger, I must disappear.

To bring us together would be an error, so do not be afraid. Only on paper dare I speak to you, and if you deem I should stop, my pen will be forever stilled.

Once, you asked about destiny, and I told you I felt destiny was a state of mind, a combination of choices. I must confess that in my journey, my choices have waylaid me. In the strangest of ways we are linked. Like two planets orbiting in space, our decisions affect the ebb and flow of our lives. Our destinies have crossed but soon must part.

Until that day comes, my beautiful princess, I proclaim myself your brave knight. I will protect you until a noble prince comes to take my place. Even now, he awaits your beckoning. But beware. Your kingdom is also filled with buffoons and boors, sharks and wolves. Choose carefully.

Forever.

Cyrano

Shannon put down the letter and stared into space. He knew her. She didn't know who he was, but he knew her. He'd been at the coffeehouse, had seen her with Gary. Which one had he been? One of the two good-looking men seated outside? Or the one with the thick glasses?

It could have been someone inside. She hadn't paid enough attention. She hadn't known she should.

"In the strangest of ways we are linked."

The idea gave her a spooky feeling, and yet she wasn't afraid. He'd said he would only write and would stop that if she asked. Still, Clint would say she was being stupid, that the guy could be a nut. She wouldn't be telling Clint what this letter said. She also knew that she would be writing back to Cyrano.

5

⟶ ⟵

Clint was having his usual ten-in-the-morning cup of coffee with Clarissa when Shannon came into the kitchen. She was wearing a pair of white shorts that showed off miles of smooth, shapely legs and a sloppy blue T-shirt that didn't hide any of her curves. With her hair tied back with a blue scarf, no shoes on her feet and no makeup, she didn't look like a rich heiress. She looked earthy and womanly and all too tempting, and Clint quickly decided to study the dark liquid in his cup.

"Good. You're both here," she said, and casually started toward the sink. "I wanted to let you know I won't be having dinner here tonight. I'm going out. And I won't need you, Clint. He's picking me up."

"He?" Clint looked back up. Shannon had her back to him and was reaching for a glass. Seeing her backside didn't help his libido.

"You mean that nice young Dr. Shau who keeps calling?" Clarissa asked from where she was cleaning a cupboard.

"No." Glass in hand, Shannon turned back toward them. "Brendon may be nice, but..." She shook her head. "No, tonight I'm going out with one of the men I've been writing to."

"Which one?" Clint asked. He knew his choice.

"Martin."

"The English teacher?" That wasn't his choice.

"English *professor.* And don't worry, Clint. I checked the guy out. Mrs. Yankoski, from the Children's Hospital, said her daughter had him for an English class at the U. of M. and liked him."

Clint grinned. As if that would tell her anything.

"He's picking me up at seven."

"It might be better if I drove you to the restaurant," Clint said. Though the man sounded all right on paper, he'd like to be along. "That way—"

"No."

Clint knew she'd made up her mind. Still he tried. "What if he's a real bore? Or obnoxious? How will you get home?"

"I can always get a cab."

"Cabs aren't always around when you need them," Clarissa said. "I think maybe you should listen to Clint. Is not safe for a woman to be out on the streets at night. If Clint there—"

"I'm not going to be out on the streets," Shannon insisted. "Besides, I was 'on the streets' by myself at night before I met John. Catching a bus was the only way I got to and from work."

"You weren't worth a lot of money back then," Clarissa said sharply. "You have to be more careful now. Yes?"

Clarissa looked at him for confirmation, and Clint knew they both expected him to voice a similar argument. He always did. "I'm sure Shannon knows what she's doing," he said. "She's quite capable of taking care of herself."

"Thank you," Shannon said, clearly surprised. "If you'd like, why don't you take the evening off."

"I just might."

He looked back down at his coffee. Shannon Powell might be a capable woman, but he had no intention of sending her off with some stranger without a bodyguard. She'd be as alone tonight as she'd been when she'd gone out with Mitch from the club and Dr. Brendon Shau from the hospital.

At seven o'clock exactly, Clint watched Shannon come down the stairs. Martin Harwick, Ph.D. and self-proclaimed expert on George Gordon, otherwise known as Lord Byron, stood in the entryway, his eyes widening as Shannon came nearer.

The man's reaction didn't surprise Clint. There'd been a big change in Shannon's appearance from that morning. The shorts and T-shirt had been replaced by a simple black sundress, her hair had been piled into layers of golden curls and her velvety smooth skin had been expertly enhanced with makeup.

Actually Clint couldn't think of any time Shannon hadn't looked good, except at John's funeral, when grief had drained the color from her cheeks and the sparkle from her eyes. That day she'd looked like hell, and he'd ached for her.

She'd kept her jewelry simple. A dangly pair of onyx-and-gold earrings, a diamond dinner ring and the gold necklace John had given her. Clint smiled at the sight of the necklace. It would make his job of tracking her much easier. Not that he was overly worried about her safety tonight. He probably knew more about Doctor Martin Harwick than the man knew about himself. He would be no threat to Shannon. She might even like him.

Though not particularly handsome, the man wasn't bad looking. Actually he reminded Clint of an English teacher. Or rather, he looked English, his limp hair a sort of blondish-brown and cut a little too long on top and too short on the sides. His suit fit loosely over narrow shoulders and looked about two years out of style. He was smiling at Shannon like a beggar before a princess.

"So glad to finally meet you," she said, extending her hand as she neared him.

"And I you." He took her hand in a debonair manner, bowing his head slightly. It was a little too gauche for Clint, but he imagined women liked it.

She looked his way, frowning slightly. "I thought you'd be gone by now."

"I'll be leaving soon," he said. As soon as she left.

Martin released her hand and faced him. When Clint had opened the door, he'd explained his position to Martin. He didn't want the man thinking him a rival. Now Martin's smile was smug. "Going anywhere special?"

Clint shrugged. "Have no idea."

"Well, wherever you end up, have a good time," Shannon said, and he believed she meant it. Then she looked at Martin. "I guess I'm ready."

Martin bowed and motioned toward the door with an overexaggerated flourish of his arm. "Then allow me to escort you to my coach."

Martin's coach, Shannon soon discovered, was a Buick that had seen over a hundred thousand miles, had books and papers piled on the back seat and had doors that creaked when Martin opened them. The car did, however, start easily, and the seat belt worked, so she had no complaints. "Impressive," he said as the gates swung closed behind them. "I feel like I'm stealing a princess away from her castle."

"No castle," Shannon assured him, though others had commented that the two-story house overlooking Lake Erie did in some ways resemble a small castle. "And the security's not to keep someone from stealing me, but to protect the artwork my late husband collected."

"I saw the Picasso drawing in your entryway. Very impressive." Martin glanced her way. "Beauty, intellect and wealth. I can't believe you agreed to go out with me. You'll excuse me if I'm tongue-tied."

"As interesting as your letters have been, I'm sure we'll find something to talk about," she said, and was right. For the next fifteen minutes, he talked almost nonstop, telling her about his family, which though not wealthy, was well-off; about his travels to England, Italy and the Middle East; and about his education, which duly impressed her.

Shannon was glad Martin didn't ask her about her education. Saying she'd dropped out of a two-year community college before she'd completed a summer session, much less a regular semester, probably wouldn't impress him. And she was glad he didn't ask about her family. She usually simply said her father was dead, she was an only child—more or less true—and her mother now lived in South Carolina. That was all most people needed to know.

Clint kept his Harley-Davidson more than a block behind Martin's Buick. As long as Shannon was wearing the necklace with the homing device, there was no need for him to actually see the car. He certainly didn't want Shannon spotting him.

Actually, he saw Martin turn into the restaurant's parking lot. Pulling over, Clint let his engine idle and tried to decide the best way to keep an eye on Shannon without her knowing. As soon as he was sure they were inside, he pulled into the restaurant's parking lot.

Shannon glanced around the restaurant after they'd been seated. The decor was nice and the atmosphere comfortable—elegant but not stuffy. After the waiter brought their drinks and took their orders, Martin asked, "Did you read the book of Lord Byron's poetry I sent?"

"Some of it," she said. "The shorter pieces and a little of the *Pilgrimage.*"

"*Childe Harold's Pilgrimage,*" he corrected. "That was his first notable work, you know. It was inspired by his travels in Europe and the Middle East." Martin leaned toward her. "Lord Byron was the essence of Gothic Romanticism, yet much of his poetry was a cutting satire, both of the monarchy and of his contemporaries. He didn't like Wordsworth, Coleridge or Southey. He despised all of the 'Lakers'—despised their opportunistic politics. Southey in turn called Byron a 'Satanic' poet."

"Satanic?"

Martin nodded. "That's how they saw him back then. Maybe because he could so easily seduce the women. Probably one of his most popular poems is *Don Juan,* and Lord Byron himself was quite a Don Juan. He had affairs with women from nobility to the landlord's wife. Even with his half sister. Have you read *Don Juan?*"

"*Don Juan,*" Shannon repeated, frowning. Her gaze was on the doorway to the kitchen. It was crazy, she knew, but when the last waiter had gone in, she'd thought she'd caught a glimpse of Clint.

"It's pure satire. He wrote it . . ."

Martin continued to educate her regarding Lord Byron, and she tried to concentrate on what he was saying. Some of the historical information was what she'd learned while traveling with John in England, Italy and Greece. Her gaze, however, kept drifting back to the kitchen door. Had she seen Clint? And if not, why think she had? Here she was with one of the men she'd been writing to for months. Why think about Clint at all?

* * *

Clint knew she'd seen him in the kitchen. His timing couldn't have been worse. It was a good thing he wasn't planning on going into detective work. Creating security systems was a lot easier than discreetly keeping an eye on a person. The way Shannon kept watching the door to the kitchen, he knew she wasn't aware that he'd moved to the hallway near the telephone and bathrooms.

Two women went by on their way to the bathroom. One smiled in his direction. He kept his expression neutral and pretended he was using the phone.

As he watched Shannon, he noticed Martin was doing most of the talking. Occasionally she would nod or say something, then Martin would continue, talking on even as he ate. Shannon looked like she was interested. She also kept glancing toward the kitchen.

The two women came out from the bathroom, and the one who had smiled, smiled again. He did nothing.

"Lord Byron," Martin continued, "was not a man who could do anything quietly. He..."

"Did you see that guy by the telephone?" a young woman passing their table said to the woman with her.

The other woman nodded. "Looked like the bouncer. Did you see the nose?"

Shannon quickly glanced the direction they'd come. She caught a glimpse of a black T-shirt, a broad shoulder and a hairy, muscular arm. Just a glimpse, but she had a feeling she knew exactly who the "bouncer with the nose" was. Pushing back her chair, she stood. "Excuse me, Martin. I need to use the powder room."

Clint knew he had to move and fast. What he needed was superhuman powers. A cloak of invisibility or the ability to cloud minds. What he got was an overweight woman in a flowered dress on her way to the bathroom.

The moment she passed the telephone, Clint stepped forward, slouching so he used her bulk as a camouflage. "What the . . . ?" she said, coming to a full stop before she reached the bathroom door.

He was close enough, he decided, and took off before the woman finished. Not even glancing Shannon's way, he rushed through the side door to the kitchen . . . and straight into one of the cooks.

Shannon heard the clatter of pots and pans. In front of her stood an overweight woman. The woman was staring at a door at the end of the hallway and whimpering.

"Excuse me," Shannon said, knowing she could never get by unless the woman moved.

"I . . . I—" The woman looked down at the floor near her feet, then stepped aside.

The moment Shannon pushed open the door to the kitchen, she saw the mess. In front of her a cook was picking up pans and lids, grumbling under his breath. Another looked her way and shook a fist. "Wrong door!" he yelled. "Not for patrons!"

"Did a man—?" she started.

"Wrong door!" the cook yelled again, and marched over to push the door shut.

Shannon stepped back, staring at the closed door, then headed for the bathroom. Beneath the doorway to a stall, she saw stout legs. "That man in the hallway," she said through the closed stall door. "What did he look like?"

"What did he look like?" the woman repeated from the other side of the stall door. "How should I know? He scared the—" She stopped and mumbled, "Never mind."

"Would you say he was tall? Broad shouldered? Muscular?"

"I have no idea if he was tall. He was slinking." There was a flush, and Shannon waited. A moment later the door opened and the woman stepped out. Her face was ruddy. "I guess he was broad shouldered and muscular. Tell you the truth, his popping up like that scared me so much, I really didn't notice all that much about him. You know him?"

"I think I do." Shannon was sure it was Clint. It had to have been him. All that bit about no problem with her going out with Martin. Sure, no problem. That was because he was planning on following her, spying on her.

She could strangle the man. Might strangle the man. She smiled at the woman. "When I get my hands on him." She wrapped her hands around an imaginary neck.

"Give it a squeeze for me," the woman said. "He made me wet my pants."

Shannon was fully composed by the time she returned to the table. She saw no sense in letting Martin know she had an overprotective chauffeur who was going to be looking for another job in the morning. For the rest of dinner, she heard amusing tales about Lord Byron, and amusing tales about Martin's experiences teaching English composition. She laughed more than she had in months.

She also kept glancing around the restaurant, looking for Clint. She was sure he was somewhere, spying on her. In Martin's car, driving back to her house, Shannon kept glancing in the sideview mirror, expecting to see Clint on his motorcycle or in the Mercedes or the Jaguar. She wouldn't put it past him to use one of her cars to tail her.

At her door, Martin asked if she'd like to go out again. She said yes and told him to call. As far as she was concerned, he was exactly what she'd expected—literate and a pleasure to be with. He didn't try to kiss her, and she entered the house alone, going straight to Clint's room.

She wasn't surprised that he wasn't there. Tailing her, how could he be? Just to make sure, however, she headed for the garage. If his bike or one of the cars was gone, she'd know for sure.

Clint stepped out of the bungalow where Clarissa and Angelo lived before Shannon even got halfway to the garage. "Home already?" he asked, glancing at his watch.

She was surprised to see him. Especially surprised to see him wearing a red T-shirt with a hole in the side and grease stains on the sleeve. "You're here?"

"Yeah." He shrugged. "Didn't get away after all. Had trouble with my bike." A nod of his head toward the bungalow indicated exactly where he'd been. "Angelo's been trying to cheat me out of all my money."

Shannon walked closer to the doorway. Past Clint, she could see Angelo seated at the kitchen table, cards dealt out for two people and a beer can by the side of each hand. Clarissa was in the living room, watching television.

"You've been here all evening?" she asked Clint, frowning, confused.

"Well, since I gave up on getting my bike running."

"Angelo," she called into the bungalow. "Has he been here all night?"

"Clint?" Angelo looked at him and smiled. "Yes. All the night."

Clint lifted his eyebrows. "What? You didn't believe me?"

"I just..." She sighed, not sure what to believe anymore. "I'm just sorry you didn't get to go out."

"So am I," he said, then smiled. "Did you have a good time?"

"Yes I did." She nodded, deciding that was one thing she could say with certainty. "Martin is a very interesting person. I'm going out with him again."

"Good," Clint said.

"By myself."

He grinned. "Of course."

Two weeks later, Paul Green came for his monthly review of Shannon's accounts. Shannon was upstairs when Paul called Clint into the den. "I thought you were going to continue keeping an eye on her," he said tersely, his voice barely over a whisper.

"I am," Clint said, certain he knew what the older man was going to say.

"And this man she's going out with? The one she met through those letters?"

"Has been thoroughly checked out. I've checked out both men she's been writing to."

"So who is this Cyrano?"

Clint chuckled. "No one to worry about."

"Whether she knows it or not, you're still being paid to keep her safe. John wouldn't want her running around with just any Tom, Dick or Harry."

Clint stiffened at the suggestion that he wasn't doing his job. "I know what I'm being paid to do, but John is no longer alive, and Shannon is no longer Eliza Doolittle, a naive child from the streets to be tutored and primed by Professor Higgins. She needs—"

He stopped abruptly. Shannon stood in the doorway. How much she'd heard, he wasn't sure.

"She needs what?" Shannon asked, stepping into the room.

"You need to remember you're no longer a waitress at an all-night café," Paul said sternly. "You need to be careful who you go out with."

"So I've been told." She glanced at Clint. "So you see me as Eliza Doolittle, do you?" She grinned and stretched out her arms. "I could have danced all night."

She grabbed Paul's left hand and placed his right hand on her waist. Singing away, slightly off-key, she danced him around the room before he had a chance to object. Clint laughed at the older man's expression. He knew Paul had never understood Shannon. What had fascinated and invigorated John Powell had totally baffled his good friend.

"I—I don't dance," Paul stammered, stumbling over his feet in verification of the statement.

Clint laughed again. "Give him a break, Shannon. He does have two left feet."

"And what about you?" she asked, releasing her hold on Paul and turning to him.

She stood before him, her hands raised in waltz position. He stared down at her flushed face, her blue eyes dancing with mischief, and knew he wanted nothing more than to take her into his arms.

He also knew it would be a big mistake.

"Well?" she challenged.

"I don't dance, either," he lied.

"Too bad." Just as quickly as she'd grabbed Paul, Shannon pulled Clint's hands into position and took a step back.

The laughter died from his lips, and Shannon knew it was foolish to want to dance with him, just as foolish as the night she'd reached out and touched his chest; nevertheless, she hoped he wouldn't stand riveted to the floor, making her look like a complete idiot. To her relief, he took a step with her, then another and another.

The warmth of his hand at her waist burned through the cotton of her T-shirt, sending forbidden messages to all parts of her body. She wanted him to hold her close, to twirl her around the room. She wanted him to respond to her.

A steel rod up his back couldn't have made him any stiffer, and there was nothing in his expression to hint that he was enjoying the experience. Only the fact that he hadn't let her go kept her going. The music played on in her head, and she danced, all the while gazing into his eyes.

He gave a grunt.

A grunt seemed appropriate. He was a bear of a man, gruff and intimidating, yet sometimes comforting. Being around him was comforting...and exciting. She clung to the security he offered and stepped closer to the excitement.

Immediately he stopped dancing. "You're waltzing with the wrong man," he said tightly. "I am no Professor Higgins."

Clint left the room without looking back, and she stared at the empty space where he'd been. Only when Paul cleared his throat did she remember he was still in the room. Slowly she turned toward him. "Maybe I am like Eliza Doolittle. I can't go back to what I was, yet I don't really fit where I am," she said solemnly. "And I keep making a fool of myself."

"You're interested in him?" Paul asked, nodding in the direction Clint had departed.

For a moment, Shannon stared at the doorway, then she laughed. "Heavens, no. He would drive me up a wall. Now..." She waggled a finger at him. "It's time for you to stop being such a worrywart. I'm not going out with men I know absolutely nothing about. I've made a few calls. Done a little checking. Actually I know quite a bit about Ed Sitwell and Martin Harwick."

"And about this Cyrano guy you're writing to?"

"Now there's the mystery." She would admit that. "I have no idea who he is. I asked Clint to check out the post office box, but he said no one would tell him anything. Not that it matters. My Cyrano likes to write, but every time I suggest we meet, he turns me down."

"Dear Cyrano," she began late that night, sitting at the desk in her bedroom. "Thank you for your advice on how to handle my accountant. It worked. Just this afternoon he and my chauffeur were ready to lecture me on my safety, and I did exactly what you'd said—I changed the subject then took control."

She glanced out the open window by her side. Fireflies danced in the darkness, and the moon was reflecting off Lake Erie, the soft lapping of waves against the stone seawall soothing. A shadow of movement in the garden caught her attention, and she glanced that way. Clint was walking alongside the stone wall that surrounded the estate, making his usual nightly check of the grounds. Assuring himself that all was well.

He'd taken off his coat and had rolled up the sleeves of his shirt. The cotton was stretched across his broad shoulders, and she remembered the feel of those muscles when she'd placed her hand on his shoulder.

Had she taken control?

He'd been the one who'd walked away. He'd left her standing in the middle of the room, her pulse racing and her heart beating a million times a minute. What had been in control was her overactive hormones. No other explanation made any sense. Clint Dawson had a great body, and she was human.

He was also not interested in her. When was she going to accept that? How many times was she going to make a fool of herself?

"Ever meet someone who doesn't quite seem to be what he says he is?" she wrote, then paused and stared at the words.

That was it. Clint was a mystery to her, and that was what fascinated her so. She'd heard him say, "I know what my job is," to Paul, and she would still swear he'd been spying on her the night she went out with Martin. Yet there was no way he could have been.

He was a complete mystery.

"I want honesty, yet like a magnet I'm pulled to the unknown." That she found Cyrano's letters so intriguing and satisfying was proof of that.

Not that she didn't enjoy the letters she received from Martin and Ed. It was just that their letters were so typical. Romantic, yes, but not all that deep. Only Cyrano, whoever he might be, seemed to understand the struggle she was having discovering just who she was and what she wanted out of life. Only he seemed to take her complaints about inheriting too much money seriously.

Only he was still a mystery.

6

"*Cyrano, protect me!*"

"*Fear not, fair maiden. With my sword and my wit I will banish all that dare tread this soil.*"

Shannon heard the clink of swords and watched her defender drive the faceless invaders over the stone wall surrounding the estate. His back to her, her brave hero lifted his sword in triumph. Victory was his.

She ran to him with heavy legs, her efforts to draw near in vain. Slowly he turned to face her, and her heart pounded in her chest. His eyes were dark, his nose slightly crooked and his shoulders broad. She reached out to him—

Then opened her eyes.

Her thoughts hazy, Shannon let her arm fall back onto the bed. The golden light passing through the veil of curtains covering her window brought her back to reality. It was morning, and she'd been dreaming. Dreaming of Cyrano de Bergerac... and of Clint.

She knew whom she'd reached for.

"Weird," she muttered and sat up. Her insides were fluttery, her heart still racing and a warm glow wrapped around her.

She could understand why she'd dreamed of Cyrano. She'd rented the videotape only a few nights back, and she'd been writing to her mysterious "Cyrano" before going to bed. But to dream of Clint?

The sense of excitement stayed with her, and she breathed in deeply. Closing her eyes again, she let her thoughts wander. She knew how it felt to be hugged tight against Clint's body. He'd held her that way for several nights after John had died, consoling and comforting her. Those nights, the hardness of his chest and the warmth of his skin had become familiar, as familiar as the clean, musky aroma that was distinctively his. She knew his strength and tenderness. What she didn't know was his kiss.

How would his mouth feel against hers? What would it be like to make love with him? The quivering in her stomach moved lower, and she unconsciously licked her lips, parting them slightly.

A clink from outside her windows brought her eyes back open, and she closed her mouth. With a sigh she shook her head. She was crazy, that's what she was . . . daydreaming about her chauffeur. Clarissa had been wrong about him being interested in her. All he ever did was walk away. What she needed to do was get her hormones under control . . . and to stop lying around in bed.

Once up, she looked out the window and saw Angelo in the garden below, hammering on a metal stake. There was her sword play: metal against metal. There was reality.

On her table was the letter she'd been writing to her "Cyrano." She picked it up, ready to toss it, then stopped herself. Instead of crumpling the paper, she added two more sentences, then slipped it into the envelope she'd already addressed.

She left the letter on the silver salver on the pedestal table in the foyer. Clarissa would take it out to the mailbox. Brushing her hair back from her face, Shannon pushed the lingering memory of her dream from her thoughts and entered the dining room.

Clint saw her go over to the coffeepot on the buffet at the same time Clarissa did. Immediately Clarissa hurried into the dining room, asking Shannon what she would like for breakfast. Clint knew it would be the usual: cereal, milk and juice. And as usual, Clarissa grumbled on her way back into the kitchen that it had been a lot more fun cooking for Meester Powell.

He waited until Shannon was almost finished with her cereal before he stepped into the dining room. "Any changes in the schedule today?" he asked.

She looked up from the morning paper. Saying nothing, she stared at him, then smiled—a strange, almost wistful smile he didn't understand. "What?" he asked, frowning.

Her smile became a grin, and she shook her head, her silky hair sliding over her shoulders. "Nothing."

He knew something was going on in that head of hers. Lifting his eyebrows, he waited.

She grinned again. "There was a time when you didn't have to ask me if there were any changes in the schedule. It was golf on Tuesdays and Thursdays, bridge on Wednesdays, the Children's Hospital Friday mornings and the beauty parlor Friday afternoons. Now you don't know what to expect, do you?"

He smiled, recognizing the truth in that. "No, I don't."

She pushed her chair back a little. "Well, today, there's definitely going to be a change in the schedule. I will not be playing bridge at the club. I'm going to the community college to see about enrolling for classes this fall."

"You're going back to school?"

"Yes." She cocked her head. "Any problems with that?"

The main problem was how to protect her on a college campus, but he couldn't say that. "What are you planning on studying?"

"I'm not sure. Today I'm going to look into career possibilities."

"You don't exactly need to earn money."

"I know."

A return to college was not the decision he'd expected her to make. He wanted her married and under the care of another man. He wanted to be able to quit without feeling guilty. "What about these men you've been writing to, the ones you're going out with?"

"What about them?"

"Well . . ." He wasn't quite sure what to say.

She smiled. "I have heard that women going to college can date. In fact, just this morning I asked a man for a date."

"You did?" He hoped it was Ed. Clint was sure, from what he'd learned about the man, that she would like Ed.

"Yes. Once again I asked Cyrano if he'd like to meet for coffee or a drink."

"Cyrano?" he repeated. "But he told you he didn't want to date, just to write."

"How do you know that?"

Clint realized his mistake immediately. He shouldn't know what she'd said to Cyrano. "I, ah . . ." He searched for an excuse. "You told me. Don't you remember?"

Shannon didn't remember, but then again she might have. She knew she had told Clarissa and Paul, and one of them might have told him. "Well, I don't care what he said. People can change their minds."

"If he said he didn't want to meet you, he must have his reasons."

"Maybe... Or maybe he's just shy. Clint, remember in the story of *Cyrano* how Roxane fell in love with Cyrano's words. Well, I'm falling in love with my 'Cyrano's' words."

"That's ridiculous."

"No it's not." Why she expected him to understand, she didn't know. Clint wasn't lyrical. He was like John—frugal with his words. Any time Clint put five sentences together, it sounded like a speech.

"When I get one of Cyrano's letters, I feel like I'm communicating with someone...someone who..." She waved her hand in the air, feeling verbally inadequate herself and wishing *she* could come up with a way to explain.

"You're communicating with someone who's giving you a snow job, that's what," Clint said. "The guy's after your money. Next thing you know, he'll start writing about his poor mother and how he hates seeing her living where she is and would like to get her out of the area."

"He did say something like that," she said, remembering.

"Sure, that's the start. Just a passing remark, maybe a supposed goal he has."

"He said he wanted to move her out of the neighborhood to someplace better, safer."

"Right." He nodded. "Then next will be how he needs some money. Just for a while, of course. And he'll promise to pay it back."

Smugly she smiled. "He hasn't asked for any money."

"Oh, give him time, give him time."

Clint looked so certain, Shannon began to wonder. Could she be acting like a sucker? It was a possibility.

"What's this 'Cyrano' of yours write, anyway?" he asked. "Syrupy, romantic verse?"

"No." She supposed some of what he wrote could be considered romantic, but she certainly didn't think it syrupy. "He writes nice things."

"Like?"

"Like answers to my questions. Like a description of a sunrise. His definition of love."

"Oh, and just what is that?"

She knew she wouldn't be able to quote Cyrano's words so they sounded anything but syrupy, but she tried. " 'To love,' he said, 'is to set free the gentle spirit, to allow it to grow and expand. To love is to yearn with all your heart and soul, yet to walk away because you know you must. To love is to spend restless nights and tormented days, and to cherish every moment.' You can laugh if you like," she said. "But that's how I feel."

"About love?" He shook his head. "Sounds pretty dismal to me. All this yearning and torment. I sure wouldn't cherish it."

"That's because you're a cynic." His attitude irked her.

"And you're too gullible."

She shook her head. "Not every man is after my money, Clint. Some might actually like me."

"Oh, I'm sure they do. The question is, which ones like you more than the money? I don't think you understand the position you're in."

She stood, pushing her chair back as she did. Facing him, she lifted her chin. "I know exactly what position I'm in . . . and what position you're in. Who I write to or see is my decision. What I do with my life is my decision."

He started to open his mouth, then closed it. Straightening to his full height, he looked down at her. "What time did you want to leave for the college?"

"In an hour," she said stiffly.

She waited for him to exit the room before she sat down again. Staring at the doorway he'd gone through, she wondered why she'd dreamed about him. He was a brooding, distrustful cynic, and totally disrespectful. He might have a hunk of a body, but he certainly wasn't anyone she wanted to get involved with.

Ever.

A few days later, Martin asked her to accompany him to an evening lecture being given at the library. The speaker would be discussing Edgar Allen Poe, his life and his poetry. Shannon readily agreed to go. Besides the fact that she wanted to see Martin again, the two classes she'd signed up for that fall were psychology and college English. A lecture on Poe, she was sure, would be a good preparation for both classes.

As usual, Clint wanted to drive. She saw no sense in that and told him so. In fact, she invited Martin to have dinner with her at the house before the lecture.

Clarissa was delighted to have a special occasion to cook for and outdid herself. "A Caesar salad, beef Stroganoff and a mocha torte," Martin said that night, a satisfied smile on his face when he finally finished and sat back to sip his coffee. "How lucky you are to have a cook. I get so tired of canned soup and cereal or hamburgers at the local fast-food joint."

"I'm afraid I don't utilize Clarissa's talents enough," Shannon admitted. "John used to like to entertain. We'd have dinner guests here at least twice a week when we weren't traveling. Since his death..."

She shrugged.

"Ah, to have loved and lost," Martin said melodramatically and reached over to touch her arm. "In your letters, you've often mentioned how much you miss your late husband. I've been talking about myself. You must tell me about your relationship with him. How you met. Everything.''

"Well, John and I . . ." she began, but Martin glanced at his watch.

"My, my. How time flies when you're having fun. We'd better get going, my dear. You can tell me the story in the car.''

Except in the car, Martin began telling her about a call he'd received from the publisher interested in his book. "All this nitpicking over an outline," he complained.

For the entire trip to the library, she heard how this particular publisher envisioned his book and how Martin disagreed. And once they were seated for the lecture, he continued his tirade, grumbling about the mass commercialization of the publishing industry and how good literature was disappearing from the American culture. She had no chance to tell him about her relationship with John. She didn't even have a chance to hear the lecture on Edgar Allen Poe. The moment the speaker stated that Poe was one of America's greatest poets, Martin disagreed. His side comments to her were snide and ongoing and loud enough to be overheard. She tried to quiet him down, but to no avail. Not even the glances of others in the audience silenced him.

After the lecture, Shannon said she didn't want to stay for refreshments, and by the time Martin let her off at her door, the headache she'd used as an excuse was real. "Get a good night's sleep," Martin advised, then gave her a peck on the cheek. "I'll call."

She entered the house knowing that he could call all he liked, but this would be the last evening she spent with him.

"Home early, aren't you?" Clint asked, standing in the doorway to his room.

"Not early enough," she grumbled and glared at him. "Were you at that lecture?"

"Me?"

"I would swear—" She cocked her head, studying his face for any signs of guilt.

He smiled. "What would a chauffeur be doing at a talk about some poet?"

"Don't play dumb, Dawson. Were you there, spying on me?"

"Spying?" He would call it "watching over her," and it hadn't been easy, not with everything so open at the library. "I wouldn't make a good spy."

"There was a motorcycle in the parking lot that looked a lot like yours."

The only reason she'd seen it was because she'd left the library much sooner than he'd expected. Five minutes later, and it would have been gone. "A lot of motorcycles look like mine. How could I have been there and here?"

The look in her eyes said she didn't know but wasn't convinced. "You've been here all evening, then?"

He glanced into his room. A bank statement on his desk gave him an excuse. "Trying to balance my checkbook."

She came closer, stopping only inches away, and stared into his room. He took in a breath, catching the scent of her perfume. His mind, however, was not on how good she smelled but on what would happen if she stepped inside. She certainly would see more than she should—his copy of *Cyrano de Bergerac,* the paper he used for his letters to her and her last letter to Cyrano. The checkbook defense had not been a good idea.

If she went out to the garage, she would also know, from the way he'd hastily parked his bike and tossed his helmet, that he was lying. It had been a miracle that he'd made it back from the library ahead of her. The gates had barely closed behind him before Martin's Buick came into view down the street.

"I don't want to be spied on," she said, looking up at him. "Or lied to."

He forced himself to remain expressionless. "Why would I lie?"

"Because..." Shannon wished she could read his mind. Clint's face was certainly telling her nothing. "Because you know I'll fire you if I find you're keeping watch over me like one of John's paintings."

"John always considered you more valuable than any of his paintings."

She knew that was the truth. She also knew Clint wasn't going to admit to anything. Her head hurt and the evening had left her with a dull sense of longing. Turning away, she walked into the living room. "What a loser of a night."

Without bothering to turn on the lights, she sat on the sofa and rubbed the back of her neck. She sensed, more than heard, Clint come up behind her; nevertheless, she was surprised when he spoke.

"You didn't have a good time, I take it."

"All that man does is talk. Talk, talk, talk."

"I thought you were looking for a man who talked."

"Talk, yes. Talk is fine. Conversation. Two people sharing ideas." Still rubbing her neck, she shook her head. "But that's not what Martin does. There's no sharing of ideas. All he does is babble. On and on and on, and always about himself."

From behind the sofa, Clint touched her shoulders. "Your neck bothering you?"

Martin's incessant talking had rasped over her nerves, tensing her muscles. Clint's hand on her skin created a different kind of tension. She sucked in a breath. "Yes."

"Let me," he said, the command gently given as he brushed her hair to the side.

She didn't object. Bringing her hand back to her lap, she let him take over, his large hands kneading the knots in her shoulders. She closed her eyes, and simply absorbed the sensation, his callused fingertips intensifying her awareness of him as a man. Her breathing was shallow, her insides coiled in anticipation.

"I'm sorry Martin didn't turn out to be what you were looking for," he said, the soothing gentleness of his touch moving to her neck.

"So am I." Though, at the moment, she didn't care. All that mattered was Clint's touch.

"He talked about himself a lot?"

"About himself and that damned book he's writing. I should have suspected as much. Even in his letters he went on and on about those topics." She chuckled. "You ought to have heard him tonight."

"I heard some... While he was here."

She imagined Clint had. He'd been in the kitchen when Martin and she were eating dinner. As loud as Martin talked, Clint would have heard everything. "It got worse as the night went on," she assured him. "Dinner was just a warm-up."

"He seems rather opinionated."

"And, of course, he's always right." She'd disliked that the most. "You ought to have heard his side comments about Poe."

"He didn't like him?"

"Hardly." She groaned in pleasure when Clint massaged the base of her neck, then realized how she sounded. Straightening, she tried to remember he was simply acting as an employee trying to help his employer, that there was nothing romantic about what he was doing.

"Relax," he said, the seductive tone of his voice at odds with her reasoning. "What did Martin say about Poe?"

"He said—"

The breathless quality of her words shocked her and she paused, trying to quell the jittery feeling racing through her. Again she tried. "He said that Poe was brilliant and dazzling, but with no heat. That he rhymed to excess, and that his poetry, like his prose, was cheap Gothic."

"I like Poe," Clint said.

"So do I." Shannon glanced back at him, only to have him turn her head forward again.

"I remember," he said, "the first time I read 'The Pit and the Pendulum.'"

"Oh, yes," she said, remembering her initial reaction to the story. "And 'The Raven.' And 'The Masque of the Red Death.'"

He chuckled. "I guess we like cheap Gothic."

"I guess so. According to Martin, Poe's works were tasteless, gaudy, theatrical claptrap. Nothing like the works of his beloved Lord Byron."

"To each his own, I guess."

"To each his own," she agreed, beginning to feel the tension in her neck ease, The quivering in the pit of her stomach, however, was intensifying.

It had been two and a half years since she'd had any problems from the whiplash she'd gotten the night her car was rear-ended. John had rubbed her neck back then, but his touch had been nothing like Clint's. Clint's hands were large and rough, his fingers corded steel. Yet with Clint, as with John, there was a soothing gentleness. Clint's hands warmed and excited her. "Oh, yes." She sighed, then groaned. "That feels so good."

Clint knew it was time to quit the massage. Her sighs were too erotic, her groans too much like love groans.

He wanted to groan.

"How's that?" he asked, stepping back and rubbing the palms of his hands against the sides of his slacks.

She flexed her neck, then her shoulders before turning on the sofa to look back at him. "Better. Much better."

"You need to do those exercises the physical therapist showed you."

She grinned. "Yes, Papa."

"I'm not trying to be your father."

"And I'm not looking for a father," Shannon said, the stiffening of her spine indicating he'd hit a sensitive point. "I know what you're thinking."

"Do you?" He hoped not.

"I didn't marry John because I was looking for a father."

"I didn't say you did."

"But you've thought it. How could you not think it?" She paused. "And John did satisfy that need, but that wasn't why I married him. From the very beginning I liked him. He was interesting and fun to be with. He also treated me like a princess, not a waitress. When he asked me to marry him, I wondered about our relationship. I mean, let's be honest, with a twenty-five-year difference in our ages, he *was* old enough to be my father. But it was never *just* that. I married him because I loved him."

"And he loved you."

"Yes, he did." For a moment, she was silent, then she laughed. "You're not going to believe this, but I was a virgin when I married John. I really hadn't dated much before I met him. I'd never had time."

Clint believed her, though when John had told him that, he'd been amazed. In his old neighborhood, by the time a girl was seventeen, she usually had a baby or two.

Pushing herself up from the sofa, Shannon stood. "I don't know why I'm telling you all this."

He watched her come around to stand in front of him. "It's because you didn't get a chance to talk tonight."

Her chuckle was soft. "You're right. You know what I'd like?"

"No, what would you like?" he asked cautiously, uneasy with her nearness.

"I'd like to meet a man who would treat me like an equal, who valued my opinion and who would sit with me on evenings like this and share ideas. Someone I could argue with, bounce ideas off of and confess my fears to."

"You'll find someone."

"Will I?"

Again she sighed, and he felt her loneliness. "Of course you will."

"It's not easy is it, Clint? Finding someone after you've lost someone you loved?"

"No, it's not easy." What was harder was finding her and knowing he couldn't have her. "You have to kiss a lot of frogs."

She laughed. "Martin kissed me tonight. Just a peck on the cheek." She touched her cheek. "Think I'll get warts?"

"I doubt it."

"Two down, two to go."

He cocked his head. "Two what?"

"Letter writers. Gary certainly was a frog. I thought Martin was better, but he's croaked his last croak. The only ones left are Ed and Cyrano."

"I'd forget that Cyrano."

"Because you think he's a con man?"

"Because he won't meet with you. How can you talk to someone if you don't meet?"

"We 'talk' on paper, through our letters. And don't tell me he's just conning me along. We've been through this before."

"What else can I say, then?"

"Nothing." Again she flexed her shoulders. "You have magical hands, Mr. Dawson. My headache's gone."

"Good." His was just beginning. Writing to her as Cyrano had been a mistake. Now he had to convince her that Ed was the man she should concentrate on, not Cyrano.

"Thanks for helping me unwind."

"My pleasure."

She studied him for a moment, then smiled. "So what did you think of that speaker at the library? Did Poe purposely self-destruct?"

Clint knew what she was trying to do. One slip, and she would have her proof that he'd followed her earlier that night. He feigned ignorance. "I don't understand what you mean."

She continued studying his face, then her smile became a grin. "Good night, Clint."

"Good night."

Shannon knew he watched her go up the stairs. At the landing, she glanced back. He was standing near the newel post, looking up. For a moment she thought the expression on his face was one of longing, then it was gone. She knew what she felt was longing. A longing for something she couldn't quite identify—something elusive and exciting.

He'd rubbed away the tension in her neck but had placed it somewhere else. He'd turned a miserable evening into one she would long remember. If he'd shown any signs of wanting her, she wouldn't be walking away from him.

But he hadn't shown any signs. None, at least, that she could recognize.

"Good night," she said again and walked to her room.

7

Shannon received a letter from Cyrano the Wednesday she was to meet Edward Sitwell for the first time. Eagerly she tore open the envelope. In her last letter to him, she'd not only suggested they meet, she'd even given him her telephone number. She'd hoped he would call, but a letter was better than nothing. Eagerly she scanned the first few lines.

Roxanne
Your words are my sustenance. Each day is brighter for the light you bring, each night a dark passage as I accept what can never be. The chasm between us is too wide to cross. Only from afar dare I speak.

She knew then that he'd turned her down again, but she continued reading, disappointment turning to dismay. Only when she heard Clint coming down the hallway did she pause and look up. He stopped at the doorway to her office. "You wanted to see me?"

"Yes." She waved him in. "Let me finish this first."

She read the final lines of the short letter, collected her thoughts, then looked up. "Well, you were right."

Clint cocked his head. "How's that?"

"This is a letter from that Cyrano guy." She fluttered the letter in her hand, but didn't give it to him. "He did pretty much what you said he would."

"Asked for money?"

"'A loan,' as he put it."

"And are you going to give it to him?"

"Of course not." She wasn't that naive. "It's just a . . . disappointment."

"I'm sure it is."

"And then there was one." Shannon shook her head. "I hope my coffee date this afternoon with Ed Sitwell isn't as much a fiasco as the one I had with that Gary Cleveland."

"You said you seemed to have a lot in common with this Sitwell guy. It might turn out better than you expect. You're meeting him at three?"

"Yes, and that's why I wanted to see you. I've decided to drive myself."

The idea did not sound good to Clint. "You haven't driven in over three years."

"It's like walking. It will come back."

"People who haven't walked for a long time don't just jump into a marathon the first time out. They take a few steps."

"Driving two or three miles to a coffee shop is not a marathon."

"Mack Avenue is not the place to conquer your fears. Let me take you out on a nice, quiet country road the first time. You could practice there."

"A nice quiet country road will not help me conquer the fears I have. I need to be where there are cars behind me. That's what gets me. Even when you're driving and a car comes up fast from behind, I panic and all the memories come back."

He wondered, sometimes, how much she did remember. "What if you panic while driving yourself to this coffee date?" he asked. "What then?"

"I'll deal with it," she insisted. "I've got to. I've allowed others to take care of me for too long. One thing I've learned from John's death, depending on others isn't a good idea. The security of today can be gone tomorrow. I'm driving myself this afternoon."

"If you let me—" he began.

She shook her head, stubbornly lifting her chin.

"But—"

"No," she said firmly.

He studied her face and decided she wasn't going to change her mind. She was beautiful and intelligent and too damn stubborn for her own good. All he could hope was he'd be able to follow her without being seen. "Which car?"

"The Mercedes."

"I'll have it ready."

By two forty-five, the sky was a dismal gray and the air humid enough to wring with her hands. In the distance, thunder rumbled like a giant bowling ball rolling across the sky. Shannon tried to quell the butterflies in her stomach, but even her legs felt shaky as she walked to the garage. She knew she had to go through with her plan, threat of thunderstorm or no thunderstorm. To change her mind now would only make it harder to get up the nerve the next time.

She also knew she didn't have to be a fool.

"I'd like you to go with me," she said when she saw Clint. "If you don't mind."

He put down the rag he'd been using to polish the hood of the Mercedes and glanced at his clothing. The sleeves of his white shirt were rolled to his elbows, exposing the dark hairs on his forearms, his collar was unbuttoned and he wasn't wearing a tie. "I'll wash up and get my coat and tie."

"No." She shook her head and walked over to the driver's side. "There's not enough time. Just wash up."

She was seated behind the steering wheel when Clint came out of the bathroom at the back of the garage. Another rumble of thunder, nearer this time, shook the air as he opened the door on the passenger's side. "Are you sure you want to do this today?"

"I'm sure," she said, the words bolder than she felt. "Get in."

He slid in beside her, closing his door. She stared at the ignition key and silently cursed her hesitancy. It was foolish to be afraid. Silly. Childish.

"You okay?" Clint asked softly.

She sucked in a breath, reached forward and turned the key. The car came to life, the engine humming quietly and the lights on the dash signaling that all systems were ready. "I'm okay," she assured herself as much as him, but her hand was shaking when she touched the button that opened the garage door.

The driveway beckoned, and she slowly stepped on the gas. Except for the knot in her stomach, all was going well. As she'd expected, she hadn't forgotten the basics. All she needed to do was get over the fear.

Clint hit the button for the gates and fastened his seat belt. "You know the way?"

"I think so." She'd spent the past hour studying a map and planning the easiest and fastest route to the strip mall where the coffee shop was located.

Clint could tell from the white of her knuckles and the rigid position of her body that she was tense. Jaw tight and eyes darting left then right, she eased the car onto the street. "Relax," he said softly. "Breathe."

She laughed, letting her breath out as she did. "That might help."

"Does wonders for keeping one alive."

"I know this isn't the time to tell you," she said. "But I haven't driven all that much. My mother couldn't afford a car, so I didn't even get my driver's license until after John and I were married."

"You're doing fine," he reassured her.

Again she laughed. "Is that one of those white lies?"

"No." Her driving was a little jerky and definitely cautious, but she was handling the car better than he'd expected. He was the one having problems. It didn't seem right, sitting up front next to her. He was the chauffeur. Her employee. This seemed too casual, too intimate.

He gazed at her profile. She looked good this afternoon. She'd left her hair down, the pale, silky tresses waving past her shoulders and barely revealing the red loop earrings she'd worn. They showed just enough to accent her red-and-white striped tank dress. Ed Sitwell should be impressed when he saw her. Every man in the mall should be.

He knew jealousy was an inappropriate emotion, but he couldn't ignore the feeling. Looking away, Clint stared out the side window at the houses they passed, and wondered if he was a masochist. Every week he wrote to her, pouring out the words and emotions he dared not confess. Every day he put on a mantle of detachment. He should have quit the job long ago; instead he stayed, driving and riding with her to meet with men who would never love her as he did.

He had to be a masochist.

A red light stopped them at a corner. The first thing Shannon did was look into the rearview mirror, her body tensing. Clint glanced back and watched the car behind them come to a stop a few feet back. Only then did she release her breath and relax her shoulders. Weakly she smiled at him. "The night of the accident, the van behind me came up so quickly, I wasn't ready for the impact."

"Had it been following you for some time?" he asked.

"Yes, but the last time I'd looked, it had been quite a way back. Then suddenly..." Again she checked the position of the car behind. "You know, it's strange. Everything from that day is still a blur. I remember the crunching sound when the van hit, and being thrust into the air bag. Thank goodness for that. Then I was snapped back against the seat. That's what got my neck, the doctor said. Next thing, my door opened and a man reached in for me. It scared me, and I screamed. That's all I remember until I came to in the emergency room, John holding my hand."

"And John told you you'd passed out from shock?"

"Yes." She glanced his way. "Why?"

"Nothing." She did need to be told the truth, no matter what the consequences, but this wasn't the time or the place.

The light changed and she drove the car forward, her actions more confident. In the distance, a flash of lightning streaked through the sky and a few big drops of rain spattered against the windshield. "Is there an umbrella in this car?" she asked.

"In the trunk."

"Good. Looks like I'm going to need it." The few drops of rain turned to many. "I hate to meet this guy looking like a drowned rat."

Clint doubted she could ever look like that. He'd seen her dressed up—her hair piled high on her head, and her makeup flawlessly applied. And he'd seen her right after she'd come out of the lake—her hair soaked and clinging to her face, not a smidgen of makeup enhancing her features. She'd looked beautiful both ways. "We'll keep you dry."

"I don't know why I care. This guy's probably going to be as big a loser as the other two." She switched on the wipers as the rain increased. "And don't you dare say, 'I told you so.'"

"Wouldn't think of it."

She smiled at him. "Yes, you would. Just as you thought of saying it this morning when I got that letter from my purple prose master, Cyrano."

"But I didn't."

"No, you didn't." She slowed to stop for another light, once again keeping a close eye on the car behind until it had come to a complete stop. "You know what fascinates me about that Cyrano?"

"No, what?"

"He's a mystery. First of all he writes Gary's letters. Why? Because of an obligation, as he says? What obligation? And why use a phony name? You say he's a con man. If so, why won't he meet with me? Why not play me for a real sucker? I've told him in my letters that I like the way he thinks, like his ideas and the way he uses words. If he's after money, he should be the one suggesting a rendezvous, not me. He should be pounding on my door."

Clint knew that was logical. "Maybe there's a reason why he doesn't want to meet you."

"Exactly. But what is it?"

"Well..." He searched for a reason other than the truth. "Okay, this guy calls himself Cyrano. Maybe that's because he has a big nose like Cyrano's. A preponderance of a proboscis that he knows will send you running."

"A preponderance of a proboscis." She stumbled over the words, laughed and glanced his way. "That does sound big."

He touched his own nose. "Or he might have a sidewinding schnozzola like mine."

Again she looked. "Not exactly sidewinding. I take it you broke it?"

"Several times."

"Well, whatever Cyrano's nose problem, it wouldn't matter to me. It's what's beneath a man's skin that's important, and I've told him that."

"Maybe your Cyrano sees himself as ugly under the skin. Maybe he's not proud of some of the things he's done in the past."

"I don't know much about his past," she admitted. "He writes beautiful letters, but never much about himself. At least nothing personal."

"Exactly."

"That doesn't mean he's a con man."

"All right, let's say he's not a con man, but someone who really likes you, someone who thinks you deserve to be with the rich and the famous and not with the likes of him."

"You're assuming the 'likes of him' isn't that great?"

"Exactly." He decided to use himself as an example. "Maybe he doesn't have a prison record, but several arrests when he was a kid. Lots of skeletons in the closet."

"Real skeletons, or figuratively speaking?"

"Whatever."

The light turned green and she began driving again. "If that was his reasoning, it would really make me angry."

"Why?"

"Because Cyrano would be doing the same thing John used to do to me. He'd be thinking for me, making my decisions. No." She shook her head. "I can't believe Cyrano wouldn't meet me for that reason. It just doesn't make sense."

It did to him.

"There's the mall." She nodded toward the block-long building on their left. "Made it this far."

Clint got out of the car as soon as she'd parked, opened the umbrella and held it above her as they dashed for the mall. Once inside, he looked around. Keeping an eye on Shannon wasn't going to be all that easy. Everything was too open. He pointed to the left. "I think your coffee shop's down there."

"What are you going to do?"

He shrugged and glanced at the bookstore to their right. "Browse."

"I might be an hour or two."

"No problem. But if you need me—"

She touched his arm, and smiled. "I'm not going to need any help, so stop worrying."

"I don't worry," he said, knowing that was a lie. He was worried. The warmth of her fingers on his arm spiraled through him, the scent of her all too alluring. Someday, he feared, he would forget and react to her touch, would give in to the feelings she generated.

Clint watched her walk toward the coffee shop, her hips swinging saucily with each step she took. He waited until she'd gone around the corner before he followed.

Shannon recognized Ed the moment she stepped into the restaurant. He was waiting by the door. He looked about as he'd described himself: average height, average looks, brown hair, brown eyes and a little paunchy around the middle. His smile was instantaneous and warm, and she knew she was going to like him. "Hi," he said, stepping toward her.

"Been waiting long?" she asked.

"Should I say a lifetime?"

"You could, but I wouldn't believe you."

"Then I'd say five minutes."

They found a table, and Ed got their drinks—a soda for her and a coffee for him. He commented on the rain and the heat, and they laughed over how, only six months before, they'd complained about the snow and the cold. Shannon proudly told him she'd driven herself to the restaurant. She'd mentioned her fears of driving in her letters to him, and how she was trying to get over it. "Every time I had to stop for a red light," she said, "my heart went into my throat, but I made it."

"This is the first time you've driven since your accident?" Ed sounded appropriately impressed.

"Yes."

"Congratulations, then."

He clinked his cup against her glass, and they laughed. He was easy to talk to. He showed her pictures of his children, and she told him how John and she had wanted children, about all the tests they'd gone through and how the final results showed the problem was with John. They talked about how difficult it was to lose a spouse and how strange it felt to start dating again.

Only when Ed got up for a refill did Shannon glance around the coffee shop. That was when she saw Clint. He was out in the mall area, leaning against a wall. His gaze was on her, and the moment he realized she was looking at him, he smiled. She shook her head, then glanced back toward the counter. Ed was still getting his coffee.

Again she looked at Clint, frowning and motioning for him to go away. He straightened, flexing his shoulders, and she could practically see his sigh. Slowly he walked away, glancing back once before he stepped out of sight.

"Sure you don't want another soda?" Ed asked.

She looked up and shook her head. "No, I'm fine."

"Someone you knew?" He nodded toward the spot Clint had vacated.

"My chauffeur."

Ed's eyebrows rose. "I thought you said you drove yourself."

"I did. I brought him along in case I panicked."

"Or in case you needed some protection?"

She smiled. "No, I figured I was safe enough meeting you in a mall. Driving in this rain, however, was another matter."

"From the size and looks of him, I thought maybe he was your bodyguard."

"I think Clint sometimes sees himself as my bodyguard. In fact, I'm sure he's followed me places. I've just never caught him, and he always denies it."

"Why would he follow you if you didn't want him to?"

"He worries about someone snatching me off the streets."

"Well, I guess I can understand that," Ed said. "You're a very beautiful woman . . . and rich."

"Which I'm beginning to consider a curse, not a blessing."

"Don't ever resent having money. It's how you use it that's important."

"My feelings exactly," she said, liking Ed more and more.

"You know," he said, "I saw you on TV once. It was over three years ago. You were wearing a neck brace then."

"From that accident. That must have been the interview after John bought the Rembrandt."

"The Rembrandt you recently donated to the Art Institute. Strange, isn't it? Back when you did that TV interview, I was still mourning the death of my wife, but there was something about you that I found very attractive. Then, four months ago, there's that article about you donating that painting to the Detroit Institute of the Arts and wanting love letters."

"I never said I wanted love letters," she insisted.

"Which you explained in your first letter to me, and if you'll recall, I didn't send you a love letter. I just had to tell you that I understood what you were going through."

"Your letter really touched me," she said, remembering the feeling. "I sensed you understood."

For nearly two hours, Clint wandered up and down the walkway past the coffee shop, pausing to glance in. Shannon never noticed. She was too involved in her conversation.

He was glad she was enjoying herself. He watched her nod and shake her head, her hair brushing across her shoulders. Occasionally she pushed a silky wave back with a swipe of her hand, only to have it fall forward again.

Ed never took his eyes off her. Not that Clint blamed him. Shannon was a pleasure to watch.

Sitwell wasn't exactly handsome, but he wasn't bad looking, and in the car, Shannon had said a man's looks didn't matter. She'd also said a man's past didn't matter.

So was he the fool?

Twice she'd made obvious advances. The night he'd found her in the kitchen and she'd touched him, he'd wanted to take her in his arms. The time she'd danced with him, he'd never wanted to let her go. Both times he'd walked away, denying his feelings. He'd done it for her sake.

But had he been right?

She'd said she was falling in love with Cyrano. "Could she love me?"

A woman walking by gave him a funny look, and he realized he'd spoken out loud. He was a fool all right. Standing in the middle of a mall, talking to himself. A crazy fool.

Smiling, he shifted weight on his feet and watched Shannon. What would happen if he confessed that he was Cyrano?

She'd probably laugh her head off.

But maybe she wouldn't.

He didn't want secrets between them. There were already too many secrets, too many lies. She needed to be told about the accident, needed to understand why he'd been hired to protect her. She needed to be told everything.

Then she could decide.

Clint saw both Shannon and Ed rise from the table and knew they were about to leave. He walked back to the main entrance and waited. Within minutes, Shannon came down the hallway, Ed by her side. She introduced Ed to him, then turned to Ed. "Tomorrow night, then?" she said, smiling warmly.

"I'll pick you up at six," he answered.

"Do you mind driving back?" Shannon asked when they reached the car.

"It's what I'm paid to do." He held the door for her.

"To drive me places and keep an eye on me?"

"I was just walking by."

"Of course." Grinning, she got into the car. "So what do you think of him?"

"He seems nice," Clint said cautiously. "What do *you* think of him?"

"That he's intelligent, interesting and knows how to listen as well as talk."

They both knew she was referring to Martin. "I take it you liked him."

"Yes," she said without hesitation. "I know you probably think I'm foolish, that I don't know him, and you're right, I don't. But I like what I've gotten to know through his letters and today. He's funny, too. He was telling me about an incident with his vice presidents..."

Clint got into the car and started back to the estate. As he drove, Shannon repeated the story Ed had told her. Clint only half listened. What he heard was the lightheartedness that had been missing since John's death, the bubbly enthusiasm and the vitality. He heard the pride when she mentioned Ed's rapid rise in the business world, and Clint knew he'd been right from the beginning. Edward J. Sitwell was the man for her. He was the one she should marry, the one who should father her children and the one she should grow old with. Not some streetwise guy who hadn't even started his own business and knew more about stealing golf carts than riding in them.

He glanced into the rearview mirror and saw the sparkle in her eyes. Cyrano would remain a mystery man, and one day soon, Clint Dawson would be turning in his resignation. Anything else would be crazy.

8

Clint threw away the gray paper he'd been using for his "Cyrano" letters, and he noticed that Shannon didn't leave any letters postmarked for "Cyrano" for Clarissa to mail. He was sure Shannon was too busy to even think of Cyrano. From that Saturday she first met Ed, she was out with him every night. They went to dinner, to movies, dancing and to a concert. On the Fourth of July, they took his children to watch the fireworks on the Detroit River, and the week after that, she went with Ed to a trade show at Cobo Hall.

Clint followed her the first couple times, just to make sure she was all right. He soon realized there was no need. Ed stuck by her side with the attentiveness of a lover, and the first time he kissed Shannon was the last time Clint tailed her.

As the month went by, Clint tried to convince himself that he was happy for Shannon, that things were working out exactly as he'd hoped. He began making plans for when he would quit and start his own business. The evenings she was out with Ed, he studied the classified section of the *Free Press* for available commercial real estate, made calls and checked out properties. His plans were finally coming together.

And he was miserable.

By the end of the month, he was glad when his day off came around. He needed to get away, needed to get his mind off Shannon. Seeing her so happy was tearing him apart. No matter how many times he told himself all was working out for the best, he couldn't stop the ache inside.

He stepped out of his room into the hallway, only to stop. Sitting on the bottom step of the stairway was Shannon. He could tell by her puffy red eyes that she'd been crying. Now she simply stared into space, her shoulders slumped. "What's the matter?" he asked, walking over.

She looked up and a slight smile touched her lips, then was gone. A shrug was her only answer.

He sat beside her on the stair, but didn't touch her. "You look like you lost your best friend."

"In a way I have," she said, studying the carpeting between her sandal-clad feet. "Do you know what day this is?"

"No." Other than the fourth Monday in July.

"Ten years ago, on this date, John and I were married." She looked at him. "It wasn't much of a wedding, certainly nothing elaborate. John pledged his love to me, and I pledged my love to him and the judge proclaimed us husband and wife."

"That's all that's important, isn't it?"

"Yes." She sighed. "My mother was there, with her latest boyfriend, and Ginny, my best friend at the time. Paul stood up with John. After the ceremony we all went out for lunch." She smiled. "I can't remember where we went or what I ate. I do remember pinching myself. I couldn't believe it was all real."

"Cinderella marries the prince."

She nodded. "That's how I felt. It was a fairy tale come true. Then we came back here and John told his mother. That's when I discovered where the wicked witch lived."

"His mother didn't approve of you marrying him?"

Shannon laughed, some of the sparkle coming back into her eyes. "Approve? As far as Mother Powell was concerned, I was a gold digger after John's money and nothing more. For two years she made me feel like an interloper in this house. It took a stroke for her to accept me. The one thing I can say is before she died, she did say she was glad John had married me."

"Those two years must have been difficult ones."

"They were. John was still running the family business then and was gone from the house a great deal of the time." She looked toward Clint's room. "We were sleeping down here then. To avoid running into Mother Powell, I spent a lot of hours in there."

Clint had thought about that, thought about her sleeping in the bed that he now slept in. Some nights he'd imagined her there again. "Didn't you say anything to John?"

"Not at first. For a while, I thought once she got to know me she would change her mind. But no matter what I did or what I said, she ran me down. With just a word or two, she could make me feel like dirt. Finally, just before she had her stroke, I told John I wasn't sure how much longer I could stand it. That's when he told me he'd had an offer for the business that he was considering. He said if the deal went through, we could move to Europe. As it turned out, he did sell the business, but Mother Powell had her stroke, and we didn't move. Her health was so fragile after that, we didn't go anywhere, not until she died. Then John took me to Europe, and to the Orient and to Australia. We traveled everywhere, and met everyone you could imagine, from princesses and princes, to ambassadors and the owners of big businesses. That's when I really learned that money can talk, and it's not what you know but who you know that's important. And that's when John decided to invest in art."

She glanced at the Picasso in the entryway. "Sometimes I think it's a shame to have them here. They should be in galleries where others can enjoy them."

"That's why you donated the Rembrandt?"

"For that reason, and because it reminded me too much of John." Once again she sighed. "Sometimes the memories still hurt."

"You going to be all right?" He was concerned. He hadn't seen her this low in months. "Are you seeing Ed later today?"

"Ed's in New York. He'll be there all week."

"Do you have anything planned? Anywhere to go today?" She needed to get out of the house and away from her memories.

"No."

"Want to do something with me?"

She looked surprised. That he'd asked surprised him, but there was no taking it back now, not when she smiled and said, "Yes, I would like that."

"Then allow me." He stood and bowed before her. "Today we will go wherever you like, do whatever you desire. Your wish is my command."

She let her gaze slide down over his T-shirt and jeans, his usual attire for Mondays. "You were going to go visit your mother, weren't you?"

"She can survive one week without my ugly face."

"I told you once before, your face isn't ugly," Shannon said quickly. It disturbed her to hear him say the word.

He shrugged off her comment.

"What I'd like to do..." She considered the possibilities, then knew. "Is whatever you usually do on your day off."

He frowned, but she ignored it. "I'd like to go where you usually go, see where you lived. Visit with your mother."

"My mother would talk your ears off," Clint grumbled.

"And tell me all about you?" Shannon could tell he didn't like that idea. Standing, she pushed her hair back and looked up at him. "I also want to ride on your motorcycle."

"On the Harley?"

She laughed, suddenly feeling young and reckless and so much better than she had only minutes before. "You can't imagine how many times I've wanted to ask you for a ride."

He shook his head. "It wouldn't be safe."

"You promised," she reminded him. "'Your wish is my command,' you said."

He glanced down at her shorts, bare legs and sandals. "Then go change to some long pants. Boots or sneakers."

"Give me five," she said and started up the stairs, a bounce to her steps.

When Angelo had shown an interest in Clint's Harley-Davidson, Clint had gotten him a used helmet, taken him for a ride and had let him try it out on a couple of back roads. Clarissa didn't like it when Angelo went with him, but Angelo did. Clint gave Shannon Angelo's helmet to wear. It was too big and came low on her forehead, nearly covering her eyes. When she flipped down the visor, he laughed. "You look like an alien from outer space."

"I feel like an alien," she said, the words muffled until she pushed the visor back up. Her eyes sparkled with excitement. "I've only ridden a motorcycle once before." She looked his bike over like a potential buyer. "Not one exactly like this. In fact, nothing like this." She laughed and looked back at him. "The one I was on broke down before we got home, and I had to help push. That was the last time I went out with that guy."

''Well, don't be surprised if this one breaks down.'' It wouldn't be the first time, though he'd been working on it a lot these past three and a half years, filling in the time when he didn't have anything to do but wait for Shannon to want to go somewhere. For as old as the Harley was, it ran pretty well. ''Ready?'' He kicked down the footrests for her, got on and waited for her to climb on behind him.

Offering to do whatever she wanted had not been a good idea. There was no way to ignore the feel of her hands on his sides or the soft throaty sound of her voice when she said, ''Ready.''

He didn't go as fast as he usually did, didn't take the corners as tight or stop on a dime. He did suck in a breath when she leaned forward to say something. Her chest just touched his back, and it wasn't as though they didn't have clothes on. Her shirt was probably silk, her bra the same. His T-shirt was one hundred percent cotton. The problem was, he could feel the hard nubs of her nipples and the soft mounds of her breasts as if he and Shannon were both naked, and his imagination, when it came to Shannon Powell, was too fertile.

One thing he discovered: riding a motorcycle on Michigan's pothole-infested streets in a state of arousal was not physically pleasurable. He was ready to get off, to put more space between them, yet their destination held peril. The one place he'd wanted to keep Shannon away from was his old neighborhood, and here he was taking her there. He also had no idea how he was going to keep his mother from saying too much when she met Shannon. As they neared the house he'd grown up in, he was torn between a desire to keep going and a need to stop.

Shannon knew Clint's mother lived on the south side of Detroit. She hadn't realized, however, that the neighborhood would be this run-down...or frightening. Brick buildings stood vacant, gutted out by fires or boarded up. Groups of teenagers congregated on the street corners and in the streets, while the older men seemed to keep their numbers down to two or three and favored doorways and more shaded areas. No matter what color the skin, the faces all looked the same. Their progress into the area was followed with cold stares and frowns. Only once did someone lift a hand in greeting. Clint raised his in response but kept on going.

She tightened her grip on his waist, glad to be on a bike that vibrated with power. The motorcycle was an extension of Clint—lean, rugged and brawny. The tension in his body radiated through her fingertips, and though the bike wasn't going fast, she sensed a touch would pour on the power, effectively taking them away from any danger.

The house he stopped in front of was as old as the others around it, but was surrounded by a wooden fence and had a look of care. Reluctantly she released her hold on his waist and took in her surroundings. A group of four boys in their late teens was coming toward them. Unlike the other groups she'd seen, these four were smiling. "How goes it, bro?" one called to Clint.

"Going well," he said, dismounting from the bike and pulling his helmet from his head. "And for you, Leon?"

"Survivin'." Leon was staring at her, but he glanced Clint's way. "You comin' to the game this afternoon?"

She saw Clint grimace. "You're playing *this* afternoon?"

"Three o'clock," Leon answered, his gaze back on Shannon. "Over at the park. This your woman?"

Clint looked her way. "This is Cinderella."

"You spoofin' me, man?"

"Would I do that?" He held out his hand for Shannon to take and balanced the bike as she dismounted. "Cinderella," he said with a nod toward the four boys. "I'd like you to meet Leon, Bennett, Deon and Hasan."

"Hi," she said and pulled off her helmet. With a toss of her head, she let her hair fall back around her shoulders. All four boys stared at her, then looked at Clint. "And I suppose you is Prince Charming," Leon said.

Clint grinned. "Of course." He pushed his bike toward a gate in the fence. "I'm taking Cinderella to meet my mother, Queen Charming."

"Yo mother ain't charmin'," Deon said, shaking his head. "She yelled at me just this mornin'."

"'Cause you stole her newspaper," Bennett said accusingly.

Deon quickly looked at Clint. "I brought it back, man. I needed to see somethin'. I was just borrowin' it."

"You know my mother," Clint said. "She doesn't take too kindly to borrowing." He gave Shannon a key and motioned toward the gate. "Can you unlock it?"

She opened the gate and stepped through. Clint hesitated before he followed with the motorcycle. "I'll try to make it to the game this afternoon, but don't count on it," he said to Leon. "Good luck, though."

"Shore," Leon said, and Shannon could tell he was disappointed.

"We'll be there," she mouthed to Leon before she closed the gate.

By the time the latch clicked, Clint had his bike parked and was coming back toward her. He locked the gate from the inside, tested it, then took her helmet from her. "Around here," he said, putting the two helmets in a closet and locking that, "if things aren't behind locked doors, they get 'borrowed.'"

"I see." She thought of the fences and gates surrounding her house. "Not much different from my place, is it?"

He laughed. "No, not at all." Taking her elbow, he guided her toward the stairs that led to the back door. "We won't stay long. Just a hello and a goodbye, then we can find something to do for the rest of the day. I've got to warn you, don't believe a word my mother says."

He seemed nervous. And Mrs. Dawson's surprise when Clint introduced them was evident. Over the yipping of a small, nondescript dog that kept bouncing up and down at her feet, the older woman exclaimed, "You brought her *here?*" She then yelled at the dog, "Coco, be quiet," and extended her hand. "Glad to meet you. My son's told me a lot about you."

Too much, Clint feared. "She wanted to see how I spend my day off. We just stopped by for a minute."

"Actually, Clint was feeling sorry for me this morning and said he'd entertain me today," Shannon explained. "I told him I wanted him to do exactly what he always does on his day off."

"Well, you're certainly welcome," Mrs. Dawson said. "Coco!" she yelled again, and leaned down to scoop up the dog. "You'll have to excuse her. She's my watchdog. Shh," she chastised, waving a finger at the dog, then she looked at Clint. "Your sister's coming by this morning. She wants to type a résumé on the computer. She sure would like one and said you should ask that Gary if he has any more to give away. I told her I didn't think you'd be asking for anything more from him, not after he went and made you—"

"Why don't we go into the kitchen, Mom?" Clint said, grabbing her arm and turning her in that direction. All he needed was for Shannon to hear that he'd had to write letters for a person named Gary who'd given his mother a computer.

Ignoring Shannon, he hurried his mother into the kitchen. As soon as they were out of hearing of Shannon, he whispered, "Don't say anything about those letters or Gary."

His mother looked at him, glanced back at Shannon, then grinned. "Ahh."

Agh better described how Clint felt. Sick. Helpless.

"Would you like some ice tea?" his mother asked Shannon.

"We're not staying long," Clint said quickly.

"I'd love some," Shannon answered and followed them to the kitchen table. She was looking at everything. The wallpaper. The linoleum. The cupboards. "This is nice," she said.

"Clint's done a lot of work on the old place," his mother said, keeping Coco on her lap when she sat. "Even put in an air conditioner for me. Can you get the ice tea?" she asked him.

From the refrigerator, he got ice tea for them and ice water for himself. He poured it into small glasses. He had to get Shannon out of the house as soon as possible. His mother had already said too much. He had no idea what she might say next.

She quickly let him know.

"So what do you think of my son?" she asked Shannon.

"I think he's very nice, Mrs. Dawson," Shannon answered, looking at him.

"He's the only one of my boys who turned out worth a damn, no thanks to his father. You know about his father and brothers, don't you?"

Clint cringed. "Mom, she doesn't want to hear our family history."

"Clint told me," Shannon said. "At least a little."

"Did he tell you his father was a no-good?" she began. "Oh, he was good looking—big. Tall, like Clint. Dark hair.

Dark eyes. And oh, what a smooth talker. Talked me into the back seat of his car when I was only sixteen. That was the first time he knocked me up.''

''Mom!'' Clint grimaced.

''Well, he did,'' his mother answered, a little indignant.

''My mother got knocked up with me when she was eighteen,'' Shannon said.

''You got any brothers or sisters?'' Mrs. Dawson asked.

''A two-year-old half sister.'' Shannon laughed, shaking her head. ''My mother thought she was going through menopause and stopped practicing birth control. Not too smart, I'd say.''

''Well, if two kids is all she had, your mother's a heck of a lot smarter than me. By the time I was twenty-four, I'd had five. Three boys and two girls. Lost Carrie when she was three. She died of meningitis, the doctors said. Had my tubes tied when Lizzy was born. Told that doctor, 'No more.' ''

''You lost a son, too, didn't you?''

Clint was surprised Shannon had remembered.

''Might as well say I lost two,'' his mother answered sadly and stroked her dog. ''If one of them inmates don't get Clay, he'll be dead within a year of gettin' out.''

''Maybe he'll change,'' Clint said, though he doubted it. The last time he'd talked to Clay, his brother was still talking about the next big heist.

''My husband taught his children well,'' Mrs. Dawson said bitterly. ''He taught them to lie and to steal. Only way they knew how to make any money was to take it from someone else.'' She grinned at Clint. ''Kinda ironic that you end up protecting people.''

''Protecting their property,'' Clint said, afraid Shannon might pick up on what his mother had said.

"My husband—late husband," Shannon corrected, "felt it was Clint's knowledge of theft that made him so valuable."

"Well I'm glad something good is coming of it." She looked at Clint. "Reminds me. Don Williams called. Wanted to know if you was goin' to the game this afternoon. He told me where it was, but I'll be darned if I can remember."

"I just talked to Leon. He said it's at the park. I told him I wasn't sure if I could make it."

"Don Williams is the one who turned Clint around," his mother told Shannon. "Found Clint all beat-up after a gang fight, patched him up and took him under his wing. Got him wrestling. Show her some of them medals you won," she ordered Clint.

"Shannon doesn't want to see my medals."

"Sure I do," she said, enjoying his obvious discomfort.

"He done pretty good," Mrs. Dawson said while Clint went to get his medals. "Most of all, Don got Clint to finish high school and go into the Marines. Now he's got Clint's helpin' other boys. Leon's his latest." She looked up as Clint came back into the room. "Leon told me he thinks you should write a book."

"Sure," Clint said, passing off the idea.

"I met a Leon. Just outside of your house," Shannon said and waited for Clint to open the box he'd set on the table.

"Boy's always hanging around here." Mrs. Dawson glanced toward the window, then waved a hand toward the box. "Well, open it. Show her."

"Yes, Mother."

Clint opened the wooden box, and Shannon leaned closer. Gold-, silver- and bronze-colored medals filled the box, some hanging from red-white-and-blue ribbons and others simply piled on top of each other. She picked up a handful and read the inscriptions. "First Place, Open Freestyle, Heavyweight. National Open Freestyle Heavyweight Champion. Very impressive."

"I used to throw my weight around a lot."

She grinned. "You still do."

A lift of his eyebrows was all she got. Mrs. Dawson was the one who spoke. "Have you read any of his poetry?"

"Poetry?" Shannon repeated.

"I'm not showing you my poetry." That's all he would need, for her to see his handwriting, read lines that echoed the ones he'd written to her in the guise of Cyrano. He might as well present her with a written confession. "We should be going."

"What's your hurry?" his mother asked.

"I thought we'd—"

The sound of the front door being opened stopped him, and he knew he should have gotten Shannon out of there sooner. If his mother was a talker, his sister, Lizzy, was worse.

"That's probably your sister," his mother said, confirming his thoughts. "She heard they're taking applications at Chrysler. That's why she needs a résumé."

"She bringing her kids?" Though he loved his nephew and niece, Todd and Jill were pistols.

"I suppose so. It's summer vacation. Don't know what else she'd do with them. You like kids?" she asked Shannon.

"Yes I do."

Clint hoped she meant it, because Todd and Jill came bursting into the house at that minute, yelling for their grandmother, and the next ten minutes were total chaos as Shannon was introduced to everyone, questions were asked and the kids got sodas from the refrigerator. What amazed him was how easily Shannon blended into the situation, laughing when four-year-old Jill teased her seven-year-old brother, then scooted up on Shannon's lap for protection. Jill's mop of dark hair was a contrast to Shannon's pale blond and Jill didn't hesitate to grab a lock and ask, "Is dis real?"

Shannon gave the hank a tug. "As real as it comes."

"My dad says," Todd said, eyeing her hair suspiciously, "blondes are dumb, most aren't really blond and they lie."

"Well, I don't think I'm dumb," Shannon said firmly to the boy. "My hair really is blond... and I don't lie. In fact, the one thing I hate most is lying."

Jill looked at her mother. "We get our mouths washed out with soap when we lie, don't we, Mommy?"

"You're going to make us sound like child abusers, honey," Lizzy said, grimacing and looking at Shannon with concern.

"I had my mouth washed out with soap once," Shannon said, remembering the incident. "I bet these two keep you busy."

"They do. In fact..." She looked at Clint. "Could you keep them busy while I type up this résumé? Maybe take them out back or something?"

"You could take Coco out to play," Clint's mother suggested to the children, then looked at him. "And could you fix my fence? The neighbor boys were playing ball on the other side and ran into it. Two of the boards are cracked."

"I should stay with Shannon," he said. "She—"

"Will be fine," Shannon interrupted, not sure if he was afraid something might happen to her or if he didn't want her alone with his mother and sister.

She watched him reluctantly go outside with the children and the dog.

9

Clint had been outside with Jill and Todd for fifteen minutes when Lizzy called Shannon to the window. "The little helper," Lizzy said, pointing at her son.

Todd was hammering away at a nail near the bottom of the board that Clint was repairing in the fence. The boy's expression was as serious as Clint's, his hammer far less effective. In the middle of the yard, Jill was playing with Coco, pulling on one end of a rope while the little dog tugged on the other end. The scene was so domestic, it disturbed Shannon. For the three and a half years she'd known Clint Dawson, she'd seen him as an employee, a protector and a hunk, but she'd never once pictured him with children.

"Todd adores him," Lizzy said and sighed. "I wonder if Clint ever thinks about the son he lost."

Shannon didn't try to disguise her surprise when she looked at Lizzy, and Lizzy's grimace indicated she'd thought Shannon knew. "You are aware that he was married, aren't you?" she asked. "And that his wife was killed in a car accident."

"He told me that." But it seemed he hadn't told her everything. "I didn't know about his son."

"Doggone shame," his mother said from where she sat at the table behind them. "Tanya was a real nice girl."

Lizzy explained. "Tanya was pregnant when she died. Almost five months. The autopsy showed it was a boy." Watching her children, Lizzy again sighed. "He would have made a good father."

"I can tell." With Todd, Shannon saw Clint's patience and guidance; with Jill, there was tenderness.

"You never had any children?" Clint's mother asked.

Shannon looked back at her. "No. My husband and I weren't able to have any."

"Clint says you're looking for a husband. Maybe with the next one..."

"I'm not *looking* for a husband." Shannon disliked the predatory sound of the idea. "I *am* dating again."

"I understand you're getting letters from some mystery man," Lizzy said as she walked back to the kitchen table.

Her mother cocked a quizzical eyebrow. "A mystery man?"

"You must mean my 'Cyrano.'" Shannon was surprised Clint had told his sister.

"'Cyrano,'" Lizzy repeated, smiling. "Yes, that's the name. Any idea who this 'Cyrano' might be?"

"No. Not that I haven't made some guesses. He's using a post office box. Clint checked, but said without a court order there's no way of finding out whose box it is." She glanced at Clint's mother. "The creepy part is, this guy's been places I've been, has been watching me and I haven't known."

"You be careful," Mrs. Dawson warned.

"I am. I don't know, maybe I should be worried, but so far, from what he's written, I haven't sensed any danger. Clint thinks the guy's a con man."

"What do you think?" Lizzy asked.

Shannon shrugged. "I'm not sure. In his last letter he did say he could use a loan, that he would pay it right back. But if he wants money, he's sure going about it in a strange way. The guy won't meet with me, and more than once he's told me to be careful of the predators around.''

"Sounds like he cares for you." Lizzy leaned back in her chair, her glass of ice tea in her hand, and a slight smile on her face. ''You have no clue who it is?''

''None whatsoever.''

''Interesting.'' Lizzy looked at her mother. ''You remember Clint saying he knew who was sending those letters?''

''No. All I knew about was those other letters.''

Shannon barely heard Mrs. Dawson. Her own response was almost simultaneous. ''Clint knows who Cyrano is?''

Lizzy glanced her way. ''I think he said that. Why don't you ask him?''

Shannon looked back outside. Clint had finished repairing the fence and was kneeling beside Todd, talking to the boy. Jill came running to him, throwing her arms around his neck. Shannon saw Clint tumble to his back, catching Jill as he did and lifting her high above as he sprawled out on the grass. Though sounds were muffled through the closed window, she could tell that Clint and Jill were laughing. The dog was barking, and Todd was still hammering away.

''I think I just might ask him,'' she said and headed for the back door. ''And if he knows...''

Clint did one more lift with Jill, then he heard the back door close, and set her on her feet. A roll to the side, a twist of his body, and he was standing, watching Shannon stride toward them.

Though the sky was overcast, it was hot out. He knew he'd worked up a sweat, and that his tussle on the ground with Jill had left dirt and grass clippings on the back of his

T-shirt and jeans. He swiped them off. "If you're ready to go, I'll just—"

"I'm not ready to go," she said firmly. "I do have a question."

The tension in her voice warned him that all was not well. "And what is your question?" he asked cautiously.

"Who is Cyrano?"

His gaze automatically went to the house. "What did my sister tell you?"

"That you know who Cyrano is."

"How would I know?"

"Good question."

"Well, I don't have any answers." At least none he could give her.

Shannon didn't relent. "You're saying you don't know who Cyrano is?"

He didn't hesitate. He didn't dare. "Your Cyrano is as big a mystery to me as he is to you."

"You're sure?"

"I don't know who Cyrano is," he said, knowing his web of lies was growing thicker.

"Coco can do a trick," Jill said, pulling on Shannon's pant leg. "You wanna see Coco's trick?"

"Mrs. Powell doesn't have time," Clint said. "She has to go now." Before anything more was said, he needed to get her away—from his sister, his mother and this house.

"Mrs. Powell *does* have time," Shannon said, and kneeled in front of Jill. "I would love to see Coco's trick."

"I know a trick," Todd said, not to be outshone by his sister. "You want to see my trick?"

"I certainly do." She glanced up at Clint. "Your mother invited us to stay for lunch."

"She did, did she?" He glared toward the house. What next?

As if on cue, his mother opened the back door and poked out her head. "My car has a clunk," she yelled. "Started yesterday. I almost forgot."

"A clunk," he muttered, and looked back down at Shannon. "We don't have to stay, you know."

Shannon grinned and rose to her feet. "I told her we'd love to stay. You also promised your sister you'd go over her résumé."

"Right." If his sister didn't watch what she said to Shannon, she wasn't going to live long enough to need a résumé. He glanced toward the garage. "A clunk," he repeated and started in that direction.

Shannon watched Jill's trick with Coco and Todd's trick, which was a somersault; then she played hide-and-seek with them, pretending she couldn't see Jill hiding behind a rose-bush or Todd peeking around the edge of the shed. The one she couldn't see was Clint, but she could hear him in the garage, banging on his mother's car, grumbling and swearing.

At noon, Clint's mother called them in for lunch. Shannon helped Lizzy wash up the children, then she washed the dirt from her own hands and tried to repair the damage the heat of the day and a helmet had done to her makeup and hair. She found Clint waiting in the hallway when she stepped out of the bathroom. He held his hands away from his body, blotches of grease up to his elbow. The smell of sweat and grease permeated his clothing, and he stepped back when she moved toward him. "Careful," he warned.

Careful, she told herself, unsure what it was that kept drawing her to him. The lure of the forbidden? The unattainable? He'd rejected her twice. Did she merely want a conquest?

Or was it something deeper that made her reach out and touch his chest? Something more primitive?

She felt him suck in a breath and felt the rapid beat of his heart. "Did you find it?" she asked.

He looked baffled, his dark gaze locked with hers.

"The clunk in your mother's car."

Through her fingers she felt the deep breath he took, and in his eyes she caught the glimmer of passion. Then it was gone, and he glanced down at her hand. "I found it. And you're going to get dirty."

He edged around her, and stepped into the bathroom. With an elbow, he pushed the door shut, and she stood for a moment, alone in the hallway, staring at the closed door. Had she seen passion or had she only wanted to see something?

After lunch, Lizzy had Clint go over the résumé she'd put together while he'd worked on their mother's car. Lizzy sat on one side of him, Shannon on the other. Clint changed several words, making them more active, and Lizzy leaned forward and caught her attention. "Would you believe, up until he was fifteen, he couldn't even read? At least, he couldn't read anything harder than 'Run Spot, run.' Now I come to him anytime I need help. He got all A's in college English."

Clint glared at his sister. "Shannon doesn't want to hear about my school grades."

Lizzy grinned, and ignored him. "Tanya, his wife, said he wrote the most romantic love letters. And his poetry—"

Clint interrupted, pointing at a section on her résumé. "You need to change this. Put your most recent first."

Shannon could tell Clint was uncomfortable with his sister's praise, but that he'd gone from not being able to read to A's in college English did interest her. The fact that his poetry had been mentioned twice interested her. She knew it was cruel, but she pushed. "Are you going to show me this poetry you've written?"

"No," he said flatly, pinning his sister with a stern look before going back to her résumé. "Don't forget your address."

Lizzy picked up a pen to add it. "Street address or post office box?"

"Post office..." He smiled knowingly, took the pen from her hand and stood. "You can add that later. Otherwise, the rest looks fine." His gaze shifted to Shannon. "It's time for us to go."

Both Lizzy and his mother protested that they didn't need to rush off, but Shannon knew Clint wanted to leave. She'd never seen him so tense. Something was going on between him and his sister. Something deeper than words conveyed.

Only when they were again on the Harley-Davidson did he seem to relax. "Where to next?" he asked.

For a moment she thought, then knew the answer. "I'd like to go for a ride in the country. Somewhere where you can open this thing up. I want to see how fast this baby can go."

"Yes!" Shannon cried into the wind. Clint opened the throttle more, and the Harley roared past the trees lining the backroad, turning them into a blur of green.

The wind whistled by her helmet, cooled her skin, and whipped her clothing, the vibration of the bike and the roar of its motor sending the adrenaline pumping through her body. Though it wasn't necessary, she kept hold of Clint's waist. He was like his motorcycle—power and danger combined. Security and excitement.

She felt safe with him, and fiercely alive.

At the end of the road, he slowed to a stop. Turning slightly, he asked, "How was that?"

"Fantastic."

She felt his chuckle, and liked the fact that her answer had amused him. She wanted him to laugh, to forget they were employer and employee. She wanted him to think of her as a woman.

Flipping up the visor on her helmet, she looked around, inhaling deeply. Country air had a different smell from city air. There was the sweet scent of the freshly mowed hay in the fields, the mustiness of a swamp somewhere nearby and the aromatic fragrance of the wildflowers growing by the side of the road.

There was also the smell of Clint.

She knew he'd done more than wash his hands and change his shirt at his mother's. He'd come to lunch with his hair still damp from a shower and the scent of shampoo and soap lingering on his body. It still lingered, and afraid she might press her nose against his shirt and inhale, she sat back.

"I love it out here," she said with a sigh. "I remember my mother dated a farmer once. I wanted her to marry him so we could move out into the country. Of course she didn't."

"And what would you do in the country?" Clint asked over the rhythmic putt of the Harley's motor.

"I don't know," she said with a laugh. "I've just always wanted to live in the country. Maybe because it sounded so much better than where we lived. I certainly can see why you want to get your mother out of that neighborhood. Was it that bad when you were growing up?"

"Just about."

"You didn't have an easy childhood, did you?"

He shrugged.

"I like your mother and sister."

"My sister's a pain in the butt."

"What was going on between you?"

"Between us?" He glanced her way.

"I could feel the tension. Something was up."

"She has some different ideas than I have." He looked down the road. "Where to next?"

Shannon glanced at her watch. "It's almost three. Time for Leon's game."

"We don't have to go to that. He'll understand my not showing up."

"Maybe *you* don't have to go, but I promised him I'd be there, so that's where *I'm* going."

Two and a half hours later, the softball game was tied, it was the bottom of the ninth, two men were out and the worst batter in the lineup was at the plate. Clint watched Shannon jump to her feet as Leon stole third base. She screamed as loudly as any of the spectators on the half-rotten wooden bleachers, but she stood out like a pearl in a pool of stones.

He knew she'd gone to baseball games with John, but at Tiger Stadium, John always reserved a private box. With John, she would have been surrounded by CEO's, company presidents and their wives. Her companions at the moment were the teens that Don Williams worked with at the community center and the few parents who cared enough to come watch their boys play.

He'd introduced Shannon to Don when they'd first arrived at the field, and Don had given him a smile that had voiced his approval. Clint wasn't surprised when Don sat on the other side of Shannon, or that the snatches of conversation he heard between them dealt with the activities at the center. Don was always promoting his kids and his projects, pushing the kids to get off the streets and encouraging businesses to find jobs for them. From the questions Shannon asked, Clint had a feeling Don had won a convert and the center would be getting a donation very soon.

"Steal home! Steal home!" she chanted with the rest of the crowd, and Leon teased the pitcher with a lead off third.

The boy made faces, waggled his hips, and Shannon laughed, the sound honest and fresh and totally captivating Clint's heart. His gaze was on her when she sucked in a breath and grabbed his arm. He sucked in his own breath, too aware of the pressure on his arm, the warmth of her fingers and the desire pulsing through him.

"Run!" Shannon yelled, and Clint pulled his gaze off her to watch the play.

Leon was on his way to home plate, the ball headed for the catcher, the batter jumping back for safety. Leon's stride seemed too short and slow, the distance too far. "Slide," Clint yelled automatically, and Shannon repeated the command.

Leon slid.

Dust was all Clint could see, then the catcher holding the ball, Leon at his feet. For a moment the umpire didn't move, and Shannon's fingers tightened their grip. Then the umpire's arms fanned apart. "Safe!" Shannon yelled at the same time the umpire did.

Releasing her hold, she clapped her hands together, yelling with the rest of the crowd. Clint glanced down at the impression of her fingers on his skin and smiled. How like her to accept those who meant something to him. How crazy for her to care.

Don reached behind her and gave him a poke. "Shall we see if we can get some donations to take the team out for pizza?"

Clint started to pull out his wallet to check his cash, when Shannon again touched his arm. It was Don she spoke to, however. "I'll pay. My treat. Invite everyone. Parents and girlfriends included."

"You're sure?" Clint asked. He doubted she knew what she was getting into. "You may be paying for everyone in these stands."

She glanced over the crowd, then smiled up at him. "I'm sure. Where's a good place to go?"

Papa's Pizza Parlor became a riot of noise the minute Leon's team and fans walked through the doors. Tables were pushed together, the group taking up most of the floor space, pitchers of soda pop were brought out and pizza orders were taken. Leon sat himself across from her. "You really payin' for all this?" he asked.

"Hey, anyone who wins a game with a steal like that deserves a treat," she said, loving the noise and the energy surrounding her.

Leon looked at Clint. "Yo're wrong, man. She's not Cinderella. She's my fairy godmother."

"You guys played a good game." Clint clinked his glass against Leon's. "Dumb move, but—"

"And not the move I signaled," the coach grumbled good-naturedly from down the table.

"But it worked, man." Leon kept his gaze on Clint. "Yo're always tellin' me a guy's gotta take chances, reach for the stars. I was just doin' as you said."

Clint laughed. "First time I knew a star looked like home plate."

"Thought I was dead," Leon confessed and glanced down at the coach. "I knew you'd kill me if I got tagged out."

While Leon and the others relived the game from the first play to the last, Shannon watched Clint. His pride in the boys was clearly etched on his face. Leon said something, and Clint laughed, and Shannon loved what it did to his features. He was a man of many faces. She liked this lighter side to him, liked the domestic side she'd seen earlier. Seeing where he'd lived as a boy had helped her understand the man.

Her glance shifted to Don Williams, and she was surprised to find him looking at her. He smiled and held up his glass in a salute. She held up hers in return.

The group devoured the pizzas when they arrived, drank pitcher after pitcher of soda pop and laughed and joked until after nine. Finally, in twos and threes, they rose from the table, thanked Shannon and left. The boys promised their coach they'd make the next game and Don that they'd be at the center early in the morning to help paint walls. By nine-thirty, the pizza parlor was nearly empty, and Shannon pulled out a credit card and paid the bill. She walked with Don and Clint out to the parking lot.

The light was rapidly fading from the sky, pewter-gray clouds and a rumble of thunder warning of a storm. Clint looked in the direction they would be driving, grimaced and turned to Don. "Could you take her home?"

"Whoa," Shannon said, putting up a hand between them. "Not that I have any objections to riding with Don, but I'm one of those old-fashioned women who believes in leaving with the man I came with."

"It's going to start raining." Clint pointed at the mass of dark clouds rapidly heading their way.

"And what are you going to do?"

He glanced down at his boots and jeans. "A little water won't hurt me."

"And I'm not going to melt, either." She smiled at Don and extended her hand. "Don't be surprised if you see me at your center sometime."

Don took her hand and gave it a squeeze. "I'd love it."

Shannon was surprised to see Clint shaking his head as Don drove off. "What?" she asked.

"Stay away from the center."

"Stay away from the center?" Her chin came up. "That sounds like an order."

"It wouldn't be safe for you."

"Don said women volunteer their time. Lots of women."

"Some women. Not you. The center is not the place for you to go."

"And where is my place, Clint? At the country club? At the yacht club? As a volunteer at the Children's Hospital?"

He stood looking down at her, and she knew those places were exactly where he thought she should be. "You sound like John."

"John wanted what was best for you."

"He treated me like a child. Made all my decisions. He..." She felt a drop of rain and looked up at the sky. "Let's go. We'll finish this later."

They reached the corner of Cadieux Avenue and Jefferson before the rain turned into a downpour. In less than five minutes, the temperature dropped ten degrees, the wind driving the rain through their clothing. Once wet, it seemed ridiculous to stop and seek shelter, and she yelled that to Clint.

Her blouse was glued to her body by the time Clint triggered open the gates and drove onto the estate. Inside the garage, she pulled the helmet from her head and wiped the water from the visor with her sleeve, only to laugh when she realized she was making it worse. "Where's a towel?" she asked Clint.

"Forget the helmet," he ordered. "Let's get in the house."

Angelo peeked out of the bungalow as they dashed past. "You're back?" he yelled after them.

"We're back," Clint said, pulling open the back door. "You'd better send Clarissa over."

"What for?" Shannon stopped just short of going inside.

"For you."

"Don't send Clarissa," Shannon yelled back at Angelo. "Tell her I'll see her in the morning."

Inside the house, Shannon grabbed a towel from the bathroom near the kitchen. As she dabbed the moisture from her face, Clint knew why Clarissa should have come. He needed her there. He needed someone around to stop the wayward direction of his thoughts.

Shannon's silk blouse clung to her skin, outlining the full, firm curves of her breasts. He tried not to look, tried not to notice how the cold had turned her nipples to hardened peaks. "Take a hot bath," he ordered, knowing what he needed was a cold shower.

"I want to thank you for a wonderful day," she said, putting down the towel and stepping closer.

"My pleasure." Pleasure and torture. He would always remember this day, remember her laughter at Leon's jokes, her yelling at the umpire during the game, her playing with Todd and Jill at his mother's and her squeals of delight as they sped down those country roads. He would always wonder what she would have said if he'd confessed that he was Cyrano.

"Clint?"

She was looking at him with those big blue eyes of hers, and he saw her shiver. He wanted to take her in his arms and hold her tight, warm her with kisses and heated words. Instead, he stepped back, giving her room to pass. "I'll see you in the morning."

Every male hormone in his body protested his chivalry, and he had to clench his fists as she walked by. Resistance was becoming a battle, the desire to reach out and touch her growing stronger every minute. He wanted her as he'd never wanted a woman, not even Tanya, and that scared him. How long he could keep turning away he wasn't sure.

He waited at the bottom of the staircase as Shannon started up. Each step she took seemed slower than the last, time suspended. Midway up, she paused and looked back.

Her smile was a clue that he was in trouble. Warm and sensuous, it curled his insides with its teasing message. He held his breath when she started back down the stairs. Her steps were quicker now and he knew he should turn away, go to his room, close and lock the door. He simply couldn't convey that message to his legs.

She walked directly to him, wrapped her arms around his neck and rose on her toes.

Push her away! his mind screamed, all the while he was wrapping his arms around her and drawing her closer. *Don't kiss her!* his thoughts ordered. Except it was too late.

He wasn't sure if she'd pressed her lips to his, or if he'd made the initial move. All he knew was her lips felt cool and soft and exactly as he'd expected. Resistance was no longer a factor, sanity a thing of the past. He kissed her wildly. Possessively.

Kissed her as he'd dreamed of kissing her for more than a year.

His hands moved over her back, bunching the wet silk of her shirt. The hook of her bra rubbed against his palm, teasing him with the reality that in minutes she could be naked...and so could he. Warmth would be automatic, his months of frustration relieved. She was willing; she wouldn't protest. There was no reason to stop.

Except for the nagging cries of his conscience.

With a gasp of sanity, he pulled back. His breathing ragged, he released her. "This is wrong."

"Wrong?" Shannon stood, staring at him, her eyes the dark blue he'd wanted to see, her lips slightly swollen from the bruising of his kisses.

"You're missing your husband," he said. "About to do something you'll regret in the morning."

"This has nothing to do with John," she protested.

"It has everything to do with John."

Turning away, Clint walked into his room and closed the door.

10

The next morning, Shannon went down to breakfast as usual, and as usual, her phone messages were by her plate and Clarissa came in and asked what she wanted to eat. Shannon gave her usual order and glanced into the kitchen. What wasn't usual was Clint. He wasn't seated at the breakfast counter with a cup of coffee. She'd been dreading seeing him, but not seeing him was worse. A knot twisted in her stomach, and she looked back at Clarissa. "Where's Clint?"

Clarissa glanced toward the back door. "Outside with Angelo. A branch is down. Something not working in his security system." She shook her head. "So much wind last night. Rain. Clint say you got wet."

"Soaked." And she'd loved every minute.

Clarissa frowned, shaking her head in a motherly fashion. "Why you take his motorcycle and not the car?"

"Because I wanted to do something different yesterday." Something she could look back on and remember. Like a ride on a motorcycle...kissing Clint.

She'd gotten her wish. In the years to come, she would look back on yesterday and remember what had happened—the exhilaration, the fun...and the embarrassment.

Late into the night, she'd remembered those few moments when Clint had responded. For an instant, she'd touched the man, knew his passion and his desire. The wall had been breached, the fires stoked.

That he'd then stepped away was what hurt the most. She'd thrown herself at him, and he'd once again refused what she was offering. How she was going to face him once again, she didn't know.

She ate little of her cereal, the knot in her stomach impossible to ignore. The phone messages by her plate said Ed had called the day before, several times. She wasn't in the mood to talk to him. As soon as Clarissa removed her bowl, chastising her for not eating more, Shannon headed outside.

The storm had left the air smelling clean, the humidity had dropped to a tolerable level and the lake was peaceful once again, the waves lapping gently at the seawall. Above her, the clear, blue sky was filled with gulls scanning the shoreline for anything edible the storm had stirred up.

Shannon saw Clint with Angelo, the two men pulling a thick branch away from the side wall. The massive maple tree they were working near looked like a wounded warrior, its limb torn from its body, and strewn over the grass were leaves and twigs—evidence of a battle lost.

"Quite a storm last night," Shannon said as she approached.

Clint and Angelo stopped pulling on the branch, Clint watching her, his dark eyes telling her nothing, his expression even more enigmatic. She wasn't sure what she wanted from him. Recognition that she existed? Concern for her feelings?

He'd hurt her. All this talk he always made about how she needed to be careful, needed to take care of herself, and he was the one who'd hurt her. With a few simple words, he'd inflicted pain.

And she was intent on not letting him know that.

Casual. She would act casual. As if nothing had happened, as if her heart weren't now racing a mile a minute. "Clarissa said the security system wasn't working. Will you be able to fix it?"

Clint nodded. "Looks like a broken wire. It shouldn't take long."

"Good." She breathed deeply, the fresh air clearing her head. Clint would be busy helping Angelo and fixing the security system. She didn't want to go back inside, and she didn't want to stay out with them. Her decision was impetuous. "I'm going for a drive."

Immediately Clint stepped away from the branch. "I'll get my jacket."

"No." She liked the sound of the word. Such power it gave a person. She kept her gaze level with his, determined to come across as totally capable and in charge. "I'm driving myself. Going by myself."

"Where?"

She didn't have the foggiest idea. She simply wanted to get away. "For a drive."

"Where?" Clint repeated.

She smiled and walked away. "Keys for the Jag in the garage?"

"You're taking the Jaguar?"

Shannon was definitely enjoying the confusion in his voice. Mr. In Control was not in control this morning. "I'm taking the Jaguar," she repeated for him.

Clint followed her into the garage. He'd been dreading this confrontation. He knew the issue wasn't which car she took or who drove. *They* were the issue. She'd offered herself to him, and he'd rejected her. She would never know how difficult that had been.

She picked up the keys to the Jaguar and headed straight for the car. He walked faster, not wanting her to leave without him. "Wait," he cried, and jerked open the door on the passenger's side as she started the engine.

She glared at him as he slid in beside her. "I don't want you along. I'm driving myself."

"What if you have a panic attack?"

"I'm not going to have a panic attack."

"You've only driven once since your accident, and only one way, at that."

"And had no problems. Will you please get out?"

"I know you're upset about last night."

He saw the confirmation in her eyes, but her expression remained rigid. "This is not about last night."

"I shouldn't have kissed you."

"I believe I started it."

"I'm your chauffeur."

"And you feel that makes it inappropriate?" The idea seemed to surprise her.

"A lot of things make it inappropriate."

"Such as?"

His background. That he'd been hired to protect her, not seduce her, and that last night she'd been vulnerable. He couldn't give her any of those reasons. He couldn't say anything, and he couldn't stay. "I'm quitting."

Again she looked surprised. "Quitting?"

He nodded. He'd been thinking about it all night. It was the only thing to do. "I only took this as a short-term position. I told John I'd work for him for two years. I'd given him my notice just before he died."

"So you stayed on for me?"

"I felt I should...until you were back on your feet. I can see you are now." He indicated her position in the car. "You no longer need a chauffeur."

"And what are you going to do when you leave here?"

"Start my own security business." He made it sound very cut-and-dried. No emotions. No remorse.

She took in a deep breath and stared through the windshield at the closed garage door. "What if I don't want you to quit?"

"I have to," he said. He didn't trust himself any more. "I'm giving you my two-week notice."

She looked back at him, then away again. Her jaw trembled, and he knew she was fighting back tears. He ached to reach over and touch her, to pull her into his arms and console her. The one woman he didn't want to hurt, and he was giving her pain. He had to swallow hard before he said, "Is that enough time for you?"

"I don't know." Her voice sounded hollow. "I guess so."

Her knuckles were turning white on the steering wheel, and the tension between them was a viable force, pulling them together and pushing them apart. He knew she didn't want to cry in front of him, and he knew, if she did cry, he would be a goner. Quickly he opened his door. "You drive carefully."

His voice was hoarse, and he was glad she didn't look his way. He feared his face was equally revealing. The garage door began to go up, and he realized she'd hit the button. "If you have any trouble..."

"I'll call," she finished for him, and touched the cellular phone by the console.

His gaze went to her neck, and he knew he could always find her. The simple strand of gold beads she wore would be his guide. Who would protect her two weeks from now was another question.

* * *

Shannon drove away from the estate with purpose, but two miles down the street, she realized she had no idea where she wanted to go. At a stoplight, she automatically glanced in the rearview mirror, but the fear of being rear-ended wasn't there. Other concerns had taken precedence.

Clint had quit. She'd turned into a sex fiend, had gone chasing after her chauffeur, putting him in an embarrassing position, and he'd quit.

It wasn't what she'd wanted.

Why had she done it? What was it about Clint that fascinated her so? Drew her to him? Made her want to touch him, be held by him?

She wasn't a woman who usually chased after men. And sex couldn't be the reason, not the only reason. She could have easily found someone more willing. Ever since that article in the paper, she'd had offers galore, and Ed had made it clear he was interested.

She couldn't even say it was Clint's looks. He wasn't all that handsome. In fact, you had to love him to love that face.

Love him.

Shannon played the word around in her head, finally saying it aloud, "Love. I love Clint Dawson."

The honk of a horn startled her, and she jerked her gaze to the rearview mirror, then to the signal light ahead. Stepping on the accelerator, she drove the Jaguar forward.

She did love Clint. The idea was crazy, yet she knew it was true. Feelings that had started as distrust and perhaps fear had turned to confidence and love. In the past three years and four months, almost five, he'd been her employee, her confidant and her friend. Last night he'd almost been her lover.

Almost.

She'd felt the desire in his kisses, had felt the need in his body. He'd wanted her as much as she'd wanted him. So why had he stopped?

He'd said what they were doing was wrong, had claimed she was only missing John. How could she prove him wrong?

The problem, Shannon realized, was she didn't really know Clint. She knew his soul and his heart, and bits of his past, but not enough. Her visit to his mother's had revealed a little, and her talk with Don Williams had given her more clues. What she needed were answers.

At the yacht club, she made a U-turn and headed the car toward South Detroit.

Clint checked the alarms, satisfying himself that the estate was once again fully protected. Unwelcome visitors would alert the police, the neighbors and anyone in the house. Once Angelo had the debris from the storm cleaned up, all would be back to normal.

Except, Clint knew, nothing would be back to normal. The storm the night before had caused more damage than a fallen branch and broken wires. Last night he'd broken a promise and had given in to his feelings. Now he had to leave.

Two weeks. It wasn't enough time.

He couldn't just walk away and leave her, especially now that she was driving. She needed to be told what truly happened the night of her accident, needed to understand the world was a dangerous place. And he needed to teach her ways to protect herself, ways to avoid danger. He'd been wrong not to do it before. He'd thought the way John had treated her—babying and protecting her—was wrong. He'd ended up doing exactly the same. He was failing her. Just as he'd failed her last night.

He should have been stronger. Should have stopped things before they ever happened. He'd seen the look in her eyes and had felt the chemistry. He'd wanted her kisses, had wanted her, and in his greed, he'd failed her.

"All working?" Angelo asked, stepping into the house.

"All working," Clint confirmed and closed the control box.

"Meessus Powell seems upset this morning," Angelo said.

Clint smiled at the understatement. "You noticed?"

"She okay driving?"

"Last time I checked, she was headed for the Grosse Pointe Yacht Club." Clint glanced at the hand-size monitor that tracked her. For a moment, he stared at the screen; then he swore. Without grabbing his jacket or saying anything to Angelo, he ran to the garage.

"It's quiet in the morning," Don Williams explained, guiding Shannon through the nearly empty center. "The kids tend to sleep in. We try to have a variety of activities going on in the afternoon and evening to keep them off the streets. Money, of course, is our biggest problem. There's never enough. And volunteers are the other problem. People either don't have the time or are afraid to come down here. I've got to admit, I'm surprised to see you here. I didn't think Clint would let you anywhere near this place."

Shannon lifted her chin at the idea. "Clint doesn't tell me where I can or cannot go. He works for me." Or at least he would for two more weeks.

Don glanced toward the boarded-up windows that faced the street and smiled. "I'll bet he's somewhere around here. Bodyguards don't just let the people they're protecting wander around this part of Detroit."

"Bodyguard?" Shannon repeated slowly.

"Yes, I mean..." Don grimaced, looking at her. "I thought—"

"I knew?" She shook her head. "Suspected, yes. Knew, no."

Don made a wry face. "Me and my big mouth."

"No, I'm glad you told me. It clears up a lot of things."

"Your husband hired him," Don explained. "Late husband, that is."

"After my accident." She knew exactly when John had hired Clint.

"Accident?" Don frowned. "I thought it was a kidnapping attempt."

"No," she began, then stopped, the pieces falling into place. One piece stormed through the door. Motorcycle helmet in hand, his white shirt open at the neck and the sleeves rolled to his elbows, Clint strode toward her. His look was fierce. "What in the hell are you doing here?"

Shannon wanted to step back, but forced herself to stand where she was. Boldly she lifted her chin and looked him straight in the eyes. "I'm talking to Don. What are you doing here?"

"I told you to stay away from this place."

"And I told you I would go anywhere I pleased. You are not my father or my husband. You are not even my lover. You're my chauffeur." She lifted her eyebrows. "Or are you?"

He stood directly in front of her, his chest expanding with each breath he took and a muscle along the side of his jaw twitching with his anger.

"Just what exactly did John hire you to do, Clint? And this time I want the truth, not another lie."

His dark eyes relayed his dilemma, and she waited, watching him work his mouth. If nothing more, she could take some pleasure in the fact that she'd put him on the defensive. Finally he drew in a deep breath and answered. "I was hired to protect you. To drive you places, and watch out for you. To not let anything happen to you."

"In other words, you were hired to be my bodyguard."

"If that's what you want to call it."

"I think that's what most people would call it. And the nights I've gone out?"

"I've followed you."

"Just as you followed me today." Except she'd checked her rearview mirror several times. Not once had she seen him. "How?"

Again he hesitated, then he pointed at her neck. "There's a tracking device in one of the gold balls."

Automatically she touched the necklace around her neck. The necklace John had given her, asking her to wear it always. It all made sense. "I assume if you're tracking me, you'd need a monitor as well?"

He pulled a small case from his pocket and flipped it open. A tiny light pulsated on the screen, and she knew how he'd found her.

She glanced at Don. The man hadn't said a word since Clint had thrown open the front door and stepped into the center. Don was watching both of them, his expression pained. "I'm afraid we're going to have to postpone the tour," she said, using every ounce of control she could muster. "I will be back."

"Shannon," Clint said, the order to stay away implied in that one word.

She glared at him. "You and I will talk later."

She marched to the front door with determination, pulled it open and stepped out on the sidewalk. She'd parked the Jaguar right in front of the Center. Now Clint's motorcycle filled the space, around which five young men of varying skin colors but similar expressions flocked. One young man was about to get on. "Hey!" she yelled, and all five looked at her.

The smiles they gave her made her skin crawl and her stomach turn. She took a step back when one stepped toward her. The door opening behind her hit her arm, but she wasn't even aware of the pain. A deeper fear was piercing her.

"Get off the bike," she heard Clint order. It was more a growl than spoken words, and she saw the effect it had on the five.

Their gazes all went to him, their backs straightening. One pulled out a knife, and a chill ran through her. Quickly she looked up at Clint. He stepped closer, and she could feel the tension in his body. All he said was, "Don't try it."

A dark form stepped up beside Clint, and Shannon realized Don had also come out. And behind him was another man. One of the volunteers.

The five by Clint's motorcycle backed up, the knife going back into a pocket. "Hey, just lookin' at your wheels, man. No problem."

"Where's your car?" Clint asked, his voice strained.

"I don't know." Anxiety replaced the fear she'd felt. Her hand shaking, she pointed where his bike stood. "I parked it right there."

She heard Clint expel a breath before he turned to Don. "They got her car. You want to call it in while I take her home? I doubt it will make any difference, but maybe. Tell them I'll call with more details."

He gave Don the car's license number, color, make and year. She stood staring at his bike, her entire body shaking. She wasn't aware of anything until she felt an arm around her shoulders. "You okay?" Clint asked.

"They took my car?"

"It only takes seconds."

"They were going to take your bike."

"I don't usually leave it on the street." He breathed in deeply, and she felt the warmth of him though she was cold—bone-chilling cold. "I'm going to take you home," he said, and she nodded. "Do you think you can ride on my bike?"

Again she nodded, and he put his helmet on her. It was too big, and she was going to refuse, but his expression was so tender and concerned, she didn't say a word. She also didn't hold on to him on the ride back to the estate. Her hands on her legs, she sat rigidly straight, remembering everything that had been said and done. Only when he helped her off the motorcycle in the safety of her garage did she speak. "The accident," she said and pulled the helmet from her head. "Tell me about it. The truth about it."

He took the helmet from her and set it on the rack. When he faced her, he looked contrite. "I thought you should have known from the beginning. It was John who didn't want to tell you. He was afraid that if you knew, you'd be terrified to leave the house."

"He saw me as that weak, that neurotic?" The blood was again pumping through her veins, shock turning to anger.

"He cared about you, wanted to protect you."

"What about you?" she demanded. "John's been dead for over a year. Almost a year and a half. You could have told me numerous times."

The fire was in her eyes, and Clint knew she was right. "I should have."

"Should have?" She ground out the words. "So tell me now. What happened that night?"

"It wasn't an accident," he began, though that was redundant. "They found a map of your usual route from the hospital to here in the van, along with your schedule. The two confessed later that they'd been watching you for weeks, planning the kidnapping down to the last detail. They even had the ransom note written. It would have been dropped off at the first mailbox they passed after you were in the van."

"And I helped by conveniently passing out?"

She sounded disgusted with herself, and he knew he had to set her straight. "You didn't pass out. They used chloroform. You know how you kept telling me you remembered this guy reaching in to help you? He wasn't trying to help you."

"And the police officer?"

John had told her about that. "Just happened to be at the right place at the right time. He stopped to check on an accident and ended up foiling a kidnapping."

"All this time..." She shook her head, then sighed. "So John hired you to protect me."

"He loved you."

Shannon looked at him. "He treated me like a child." When he didn't say anything, she went on. "And I let him." Glancing toward the empty spot where the Jaguar should be, she sighed again. "Maybe I am a child. What do I do about the Jag?"

"Don will have called it in. I'll follow up." He doubted they'd see the car again. By now it was parts.

"I'm going inside."

"You okay?" He was worried. There was no life in her eyes.

"No, I'm not okay," she said, her chin coming up slightly. "I've been lied to, threatened and had my car stolen. I don't know who to trust and who to fear. I need some time to think."

She started for the door, and he called out her name. Stopping, she looked back at him. "I'm sorry," he said.

"So am I," she replied and walked on.

11

Shannon didn't speak to Clarissa but went straight to her bedroom. Standing in front of the dresser mirror, she stared at her reflection. Around her neck was the necklace she'd worn every day since John had given it to her. Each of the gold beads looked the same, yet Clint had said one contained a tracking device, had shown her the monitor.

She took off the necklace and dropped it onto her dresser. John had lied to her; Clint had lied to her. Most of all, she'd lied to herself.

She'd known Clint's role in her life. She'd told John and she'd told Clint that she wanted the truth, but that wasn't true. From the very beginning, she'd wanted the fairy tale, the Eliza Doolittle story—the Cyrano. She'd thought she'd grown up, but had she?

Shannon walked over to the window Clarissa had left open. The air coming into the room was warm, the breeze gentle and the smells refreshing. Gulls hovering over the lake screamed and scolded, while speedboats cut long Vs across the murky water and colorful sailboats glided along the shoreline.

All looked so peaceful. A world without cares.

It, too, was a lie.

For over ten years, she'd been living in her fairyland. Cinderella in her castle. John had taken her from the poverty she'd known since birth and had been her father image and Prince Charming. Less than an hour ago, she'd met reality. The poverty, anger and desperation were still out there. Her car had been stolen, her safety threatened. She'd thought herself in control; now she felt violated.

Her legs were still shaking, and she went and sat on the edge of the bed. Numbly she let her mind replay everything, from her hesitation when she first drove into the area where Don had said the Center was located to Clint's concerned look when she'd left him in the garage. How long she sat there, she wasn't sure, but Clarissa's knock on her door startled her.

"You want lunch, Meessus Powell?" she asked.

"No—no thank you." She couldn't have eaten if she'd had to.

The trembling in her legs slowly subsided. Clint had been right. She shouldn't have gone to the center. Certainly not alone, driving a Jaguar. She had more sense than that.

Or so she'd thought.

She'd gone to learn more about Clint, and perhaps to show him she could. Well, she'd learned a lot about Clint Dawson. She'd learned he'd been deceiving her for over three years.

Deceiving. Lying. Following her.

"He *was* at that restaurant," she said, remembering her dinner with Martin. Had he also followed her on her dates with Ed?

Ready to do battle, she stormed down the stairs. Clint's bedroom door was open, and she could hear water running in his bathroom. Without hesitation, she marched into the room. "Clint Dawson," she said, loud and clear. "I want to talk to you."

The bathroom door opened slowly, and Clarissa stepped out, a sponge in one hand. "He is not here, Meessus Powell."

"Then where is he?"

"He go to the police station," Clarissa said meekly. "Five, ten minutes ago. Says he needs to sign papers."

Of course. Clint was reporting her stolen car. He'd said he would. Here she was, ready to take his head off, and he was helping her. The man was so confusing.

Shannon turned to leave his room, then stopped. The drawer to his desk was half-open, its contents visible. One envelope in particular caught her attention. Walking over, she pulled it out and stared at the address on the front. The handwriting was hers, the postmarked stamp showing it had been mailed.

Slowly she removed the letter from inside.

Clint stared at the two empty parking spots in the garage. Early that morning, the Jaguar and Mercedes had been parked in those places. He'd expected to return and find the Jaguar gone. He'd spent the past two hours filling out papers and answering questions about its disappearance. It was the absence of the Mercedes that bothered him.

"Angelo!" he called, the moment he saw the older man working in a corner of the yard. "Where'd Mrs. Powell go?"

Angelo shrugged, gesturing with his hands in the air. "She just drive off."

"When?"

"About an hour ago...maybe two."

"Did she say where she was going?"

Angelo shook his head. "Maybe Clarissa knows."

* * *

Clarissa kept twisting the towel in her hands and shaking her head as she answered him. "She was very angry. She take a letter from your desk, call you a lot of names, then make a phone call."

"Do you know who she called?"

"No." Clarissa kept shaking her head. "Afterward, she says she's gonna have Angelo drive her someplace. But when Angelo comes in, he says she just go to the garage and drive off herself."

"And she didn't say where that someplace was?"

"No." Clarissa continued shaking her head and wringing the towel. "She take the letter with her, though. I didn't say anything. She was so angry."

He'd bet. And he was quite sure, without even looking, what letter it was she had. Her last letter to him...or rather, to Cyrano. He'd been a fool to keep them in his room.

With slim hope, he pulled the monitor from his pocket and flipped it open. As he'd expected, the blinking light showed Shannon in the house. She'd taken off the necklace, and he was on his own.

His guess was she'd head for the post office where his sister had her box.

"I hope you don't mind sitting out here, watching my car," Shannon said, feeling a little silly about asking Lizzy to stay outside. "Losing one today is enough for me."

"No problem," Lizzy insisted, shifting her weight on the cement steps in front of her two-story house. "Besides, this gives the kids a chance to play out front."

Jill rode by on a bright yellow plastic three-wheeler while Todd wove his minibike from side to side farther on down the sidewalk. Other children were out playing, most of them older than Todd or Jill. Whenever hers got too far away, Lizzy called them back.

"I should have realized what you were trying to tell me yesterday," Shannon said.

"I didn't want to come out and spill everything, but I felt you should know. I hoped he would tell you. Actually, I'm the one who started this whole mess—I mean, beyond what that creep Gary Cleveland coerced him into doing. The 'Cyrano' letter, the first one you got, I mailed that. He'd tossed it into one of Mom's wastebaskets, and I just happened to pull it out and read it. I'd suspected he was in love with you from things he'd said, but when I read that..." She sighed. "Blame it on the romantic in me, but I had to send it to you."

"Maybe you should have left it in the wastebasket." Shannon still didn't know what was a lie or the truth.

"Maybe I should have," Lizzy said and frowned. "Don't hurt him."

"You're telling me not to hurt him?" Shannon stood. "We're talking about the guy who's been lying to me for over three years."

"He's felt he needed to protect you."

"From what? Life? You know what else I found in his drawer? Reports on two of the men I've dated. He probably knows more about Martin and Ed than their mothers do."

"Clint thinks you should marry Ed."

"Oh, he does, does he? The way he's planning my life, he probably has the wedding date set. I wonder if he's told Ed?" Shannon stalked down the steps, then paused and looked back at Lizzy. "Your brother can take his—"

Shannon saw Jill wheeling down the sidewalk toward them and decided it was better not to say what Clint could do or where he could put it. Curtly she nodded at Lizzy.

"Thank you for being honest with me. Too bad Clint didn't learn that trait."

"He go looking for you, I think," Clarissa said, her expression worried. "He grumble, like a bear."

Shannon could just imagine Clint grumbling and growling like a big grizzly bear. Well, the bear was about to meet the tiger. She'd certainly snarled at Lizzy. Shannon looked at Clarissa. "I want you and Angelo to take the rest of the afternoon off. Afternoon and night. You can either go somewhere or stay in the bungalow, but I don't want you in or near this house."

"But what about dinner?"

"After I'm through with Clint, he may be dinner."

Clarissa's eyes grew wider, and Shannon waved a hand toward the back door. "Just go. Trust me, you don't want to be around when he arrives."

Shannon went back into Clint's room as soon as Clarissa was out of the house. Systematically she went through each of his drawers, finding more of the letters she'd written to Cyrano, along with some of his poetry and a series of short stories about life on the streets. Once she'd thought he'd written those stories for his niece and nephew; now she knew he used them to teach the boys he worked with to read, the simple sentences and stark imagery expressing the life they knew.

She also knew why he hadn't wanted her to see any of his poetry. If she had, she would have easily recognized the similarities to the Cyrano letters. Poignantly austere or sweetly romantic, the poems described the life he had lived and the love he had lost.

Or was it a love he longed to know?

When she heard the back door open, then close, she tensed. Setting the papers on his desk, she turned to face the hallway.

Clint walked past his room without looking in, his gaze directed up the stairs. He wasn't wearing his jacket or tie, and his shirtsleeves had been rolled to his elbows. His hair was mussed from wearing a helmet, and his jaw tense.

"Shannon!" he called out.

Ignoring the butterflies in her stomach, she answered. "Ah, brave Cyrano. Come home from another day of battle."

He froze in his steps and slowly turned to face her. She could tell how quickly he assessed the situation, his gaze darting to the open drawers, to the papers she'd piled on his desk, then to her face. "I saw Clarissa outside," he said tersely, stepping into his room. "She said you were upset."

"Upset?" The word hardly described the turmoil within her.

Again his gaze darted to the papers on his desk. "I suppose I should explain."

"This I am dying to hear. Do I get lie A, B or C?"

"I never meant to lie to you."

"I don't even believe that."

"There were certain things I couldn't tell you, that John asked me not to tell you. After that, it sort of got away from me."

"That's an understatement."

"I went over to my sister's. She said you'd been there. How much did she tell you?"

"Enough." And not nearly enough.

"The truth is, I shouldn't have done it."

"No, you shouldn't have." She would agree with that.

"I suppose you want me packed and out of here by tonight." He stood tall and stoic, no emotions showing.

Earlier she had wanted him gone. She'd been furious then. Now she wasn't sure what she wanted, except, perhaps, to understand. "Is that what you do? Write a few love letters, tell a few lies, then take off?"

"No."

She held up one of the letters she'd written to Cyrano. "Was it all a game?"

His dark eyes were locked with hers, and she saw the pain. "No," he said again, this time very softly.

She took a step forward, closer to him. "Why did you do it?"

He didn't answer, and she took another step closer. "You must have laughed yourself silly when I told you I was falling in love with Cyrano's words."

"I wasn't laughing," he said seriously. "I never meant for that to happen. I just . . ."

"Just what?" she demanded when he didn't finish. Another step put her within inches of him. "What other excuse do you have?"

Shannon saw his chest expand, and watched him press his lips together. He wasn't going to answer. Lizzy had given her a reason, but Shannon knew if she wanted to hear it from Clint, she was going to have to force it from him.

His eyes widened when she touched his chest and deftly unbuttoned a button on his shirt. "Shannon?"

Her name was half question, half warning, and she smiled and released another button. "You could have seduced me last night. Why didn't you?"

His gaze dropped to her hands, another button going. "You didn't know what you were doing last night. You don't know what you're doing now."

"That's right," she agreed. "I don't have the slightest idea what I'm doing." Another button was freed, his shirt beginning to gape, exposing his broad chest and the hairs covering it. "It all started when I said too much to that reporter and got all those letters from men I didn't even know. Except it seems I did know one, or rather, he knew me. Knew me well enough to entice me to write back."

"I didn't want to write those letters for Gary," he argued.

"So your sister said." Shannon pulled the tails of his shirt loose from his pants, undoing the last button. He continued eyeing her. "She also said you'd thrown away the first letter I received from Cyrano, that she retrieved it and mailed it."

"Seeing that letter in your hand was a shock to me," he said.

"I bet." She started on his belt buckle. Immediately his hand covered hers, stopping her. She looked up at his face. "You kept it going, Clint. You didn't have to answer my letter to Cyrano."

"You were looking for answers, for a friend."

She nodded, knowing he was right. "And in those letters, I was finding answers . . . and a friend. But it went beyond that, didn't it, Clint?" Over time, the words had become more intimate, more loving. "Those letters truly became love letters, didn't they? I ask you again. Was it all a game?"

She could feel him suck in a breath, and his fingers tightened around hers. Would he tell her the truth this time, confess what she knew?

He spoke so quietly, she barely heard his no.

Shannon released the breath she'd been holding, studying his face. "In the story, Roxane is in love with another, and Cyrano has a big nose. There was no one in your way, Clint, and I've never thought your nose was that bad."

"What could I give you?" he asked. "I have no money to speak of, my family has so many skeletons that the closets rattle and my friends ride motorcycles. John may be dead, but he took you beyond me, Shannon."

"In your opinion."

"Be realistic."

"I'm not a very realistic person, remember. I'm Cinderella, Eliza Doolittle...Roxane. I write letters to some guy who calls himself Cyrano, fall in love with his words. And I feel guilty because I'm also falling in love with my chauffeur."

"Shannon." He groaned her name, shaking his head. "Ed is the kind of person you should fall in love with. He can give you what you need."

"Can he?" She touched Clint's chest with her free hand, rubbing her fingers over springy hairs and taut muscles. Muscles within her own body grew taut, a longing developing within the core of her, one she knew only he could satisfy. "Ed's never made me feel as I do with you. Never have I had a burning desire to make love with him."

Clint knew that desire—it was blazing in him at the moment. He closed his eyes, afraid he might give in. "Shannon, don't do this. I've been able to walk away in the past, but I'm not made of steel."

"No, you're not, and today, when I saw that guy pull out that knife, I was scared. Not for me, but for you." Her hand moved over his heart. "Don't walk away again. Don't deny what you feel, what I feel. Make love to me, Clint."

He opened his eyes, and looked into hers. They were the blue of passion, of want and desire. In his letters, he'd poured out his heart. Now she was asking for more. He glanced toward the door. "Clarissa? Angelo?"

"I told them to stay away."

"You planned this?"

"I'm either making love with you or strangling you. One way or the other, I didn't want any witnesses."

He felt his jaw relax into a smile, and he released his hold on her hand to brush her hair back from her face. "Are you sure this is the better choice?"

She kept watching him, but he sensed her relaxing a little, and finally she smiled. "I'll tell you later."

"It's wrong, you know."

"No, I don't know that. You keep telling me it's wrong, but then, you've been known to lie."

"I promised John that I would protect you."

"John died a year and a half ago." She slid her hands up his chest to his shoulders, her palms warm and her touch gentle. "Clint," she said softly.

"What?"

"You talk too much."

He chuckled, in spite of himself, and wrapped his arms around her, drawing her close and up on her tiptoes. "Oh, Shannon. What am I going to do with you?"

"You're going to make love to me . . . with me."

"You keep saying it, and I will."

Her hands moved on to the back of his head, and she drew his face closer. "You're going to make love to me," she repeated, and he knew he was.

The night before he'd given in to her kisses. Sanity had escaped him. As he lowered his mouth to hers, he knew exactly what he was doing and why. In his arms was the woman he loved. She was beauty and joy, truth and hope, and he wanted to be a part of her.

Eyes open, she kissed him, and he was glad to know the lies were gone, the deception over. Yet he was also afraid to believe what was happening was true, afraid to close his own eyes or stop touching her.

He stroked her hair, running his fingers through its silky thickness; he tasted her lips, using his tongue to invade her mouth. The eagerness of her response aroused him, his need for her both physical and emotional. "Shannon," he groaned, not sure he could restrain himself. "I don't think—"

"Don't think," she ordered, her hands once again going to his belt. "Don't talk, and don't think."

He knew what she was doing, but this time he didn't stop her. Her hand brushed against the hardness of his arousal, bringing him pleasure and misery. The loosening of a button, then the lowering of a zipper exposed the degree of his desire. "Oh," he groaned when she touched him.

His breathing ragged, he pulled his mouth from hers and looked down at her. "Are you sure?"

"As sure as I've ever been about anything."

He knew he should take it slowly, should savor every moment, but too many months of wanting had taken their toll. The door was closed, her T-shirt went over her head, her bra to the floor and her shorts and panties lay in a pile within seconds. His own shirt, already unbuttoned by her persistence, was easily discarded, the rest of his clothing off before he carried her to his bed.

Only after he'd pulled back the covers, laying her carefully on the sheet and positioning himself over her, did he pause to gaze at her beauty and marvel at what was happening. "I meant every word in those letters," he confessed, wishing he could tell her now how much he loved her. The feelings were too intense to put into words.

"In the past few months, I've fallen in love with two men," she said, running her fingers up and down his arms and gazing into his eyes. "One held me close late at night while I cried for a man who had died, drove me places and watched over me. The other wrote beautiful passages and words of guidance."

"I wanted to help you, wanted to take the pain away."

Her hands explored his chest, traveling down to his abdomen, her eyes growing darker in color. He sucked in a breath when she moved her fingers lower to touch him. "You wield a mighty sword, Cyrano."

"The word is mightier than the sword."

She chuckled seductively. "Trust me, it's not words I want."

Nor did he. Quickly he looked at his night stand. "I don't know if I have any protection."

She stopped him from opening the drawer. "For more than three years now, you've been protecting me. From danger, from myself and from you. Tonight, I don't want any protection, I want you."

"It's too great a chance."

She didn't argue, simply drew his head down to hers. Kisses silenced his protests, caresses expressing what words could not. He explored her softness, and knew her readiness. When she arched her back, bringing her body against his, he knew he couldn't refuse anything she wanted. Gently at first, then with more intensity, he penetrated her, always watching her, ready to stop yet not quite sure he could stop.

Shannon didn't close her eyes until he was deep inside of her. Only then did she let the feelings flow through her, savoring the moment, afraid it would never come again. She'd gotten him to confess his love, had played on his needs as a man to get him into bed, but would she be able to hold him afterward?

His rhythm increased, actions and emotions blending. The intensity was riveting, and she found herself holding her breath, waiting for the moment when he would explode within her.

Love was a verb, and it was also a man. He was strong and tender, exhilarating and protective. The feelings surrounding her and filling her were incredible, and she knew he was one with her, in body and spirit. Only when he stopped moving did she feel a breach. "No, I shouldn't," he cried out, tensing in her arms.

"Yes, you should," she ordered, knowing his pleasure would be hers.

With a guttural cry, he moved from protector to lover.

12

—◆━◆—

Clint collapsed beside her, curling her against his body. Shannon felt the dampness of his skin and the rapid rise and fall of his breathing. Her own breathing was as ragged, her energy drained. Only slowly did the reality of what they had done push away the euphoria. She'd gotten him to admit that he loved her, had seduced him into making love with her, but they had a long way to go.

She waited, saying nothing, content to lie beside him. Finally he spoke. "Now what?" he asked, voicing her own concerns.

"Now we need to talk," she said, though she wasn't sure what to say.

He responded first. "That never should have happened, but I'm not going to say I'm sorry it did. You can't imagine how many nights I've lain in this bed, knowing you were upstairs—"

He didn't finish, and she rolled toward him. "I've spent a lot of nights upstairs, thinking of you down here. Wishing. Imagining." She grinned. "What a waste of time when we could have been doing this."

She felt his chuckle, the vibration playing through her fingers. "So is that what you want of me, a lover?"

"Yes . . . and more."

"You going to take me to the club and show me off? Or will this be hush-hush, speculated upon but never really known?"

"The club members are already speculating. If they see me with you, it will merely be a confirmation. But why take you to the club, when I'm not comfortable there myself?"

"Oh, Shannon." His gaze caressed her face, his callus-roughened fingers touching her cheek. "John gave you so much. Money. Social position. What can I give you?"

"Your love." She had to make him understand. "Your friendship. And..." She laughed at the irony. "Maybe your protection."

For a moment, his smile warmed her and gave her hope that everything might work out all right; then a frown wiped away the smile. "I haven't done a very good job of that lately," he said. "I should have told you about the kidnapping attempt a long time ago, should have been teaching you ways to protect yourself. It was selfishness on my part. I wanted to be your protector, wanted to think you needed me, at least for that."

"I've needed you for a long time, and not just as a bodyguard. When John died—"

"John." Clint shook his head. "Two days before he died, he asked me to protect you. I don't think this is what he had in mind."

She was certain it wasn't. "John wouldn't have hired you in the first place if he'd thought there was a chance I'd be interested in you. He was a very jealous man."

"I can't say I blame him."

"He also didn't understand me," she said, the realization difficult to accept. "Or he never would have lied to me about your position."

"You'd said you didn't want a bodyguard."

"Because I saw no reason for one. Had John told me the accident wasn't an accident, if he'd been honest with me—"

"He didn't think you could handle it."

"No, he didn't, and you know why? Because he saw me as a child. Is that how you see me, Clint?"

His gaze slipped to her chest, her breasts exposed to his view. She knew from the look in his eyes that he wasn't thinking of her as a child, and his smile confirmed it. She wasn't prepared when he said, "Not now. But when I first met you—"

She had acted like a child. "I was a twenty-five-year-old brat, not talking to you, leaving money lying around so you could steal it and going into your room and through your things." But there'd been a reason. "I was afraid of you."

"Afraid of me?"

She ran a hand across his chest to his arm, the muscling of his body so clearly defined. Physically he had always awed her, but her initial reaction had been more guttural. Then she hadn't understood. Now she did. "I think I was afraid I might be attracted to you."

"You had John."

Shannon knew Clint still didn't recognize his appeal. "I had John, and I loved him. He'd fulfilled all my childhood dreams. He pampered and protected me. In a fairy-tale world I would have been satisfied. In reality, I wasn't. Even before my car was rear-ended, I was tiring of the country club and the yacht club scenes and of all the frivolous social functions we attended. Traveling had lost its appeal, and sometimes late at night, when John was asleep and I couldn't sleep, I would get up and stare out at the lake and wonder if there wasn't more to life. After John died, the question bothered me more than ever. You helped those nights you let me talk. Writing those letters helped."

Scowling, she tapped the center of Clint's chest. "You are so two-faced, telling me Cyrano was a con man, calling his words syrupy."

"What did you expect me to say?"

She paused, then nodded. "Exactly that."

"I could tell from the letters you'd written Gary that you were still struggling for answers. I wrote the first letter as Cyrano the night you met Gary and were so disappointed. I'd almost kissed you that night in the kitchen, and I knew I had to keep my distance. Yet I wanted to let you know I was there if you needed someone to share ideas with. Writing to you, it...I..." He stopped and shook his head. "It was a mistake."

"Or fate." She hoped the powers drawing them together had more than a one-night stand in mind. "Stay, Clint. Here. In this house. Start your own security business if you want, but stay."

"I'm not sure I could have ever left."

Clint stayed, and the next few months brought several changes in Shannon's life. By October, she was midway through her two classes at the community college and enjoying both. Clint was teaching her basic self-defense, and driving maneuvers she'd only seen in movies. She'd bought a less ostentatious car to drive to the college, and kept a low profile. As far as anyone knew, she was a widow, returning to school to get a degree and struggling to make ends meet, just like any other student.

Clint slept with her in her bed, but he kept his things in the room downstairs. The uniform was a thing of the past, but she knew he didn't see himself as her equal, and as time went by, he spent more and more time away from the estate. He told her he was looking for an office to rent so he could start his security systems business, yet when she asked how things were going, he always hedged the question. She knew he also spent a lot of time at the center.

They'd vowed to be truthful with each other, but she wondered if Clint knew how to be truthful . . . or, for that matter, if she did. Though he said he loved her almost daily, she sensed he was uneasy with their relationship, and the subject of marriage never came up. Their relationship was too fragile for her to reveal her secret, yet she knew it was only a matter of time before he would guess.

She'd been lucky and hadn't experienced any morning sickness, and she'd explained away the tiredness by blaming it on her classes and the studying she was doing. She wanted the baby. It was Clint's reaction she feared. While growing up, she'd often heard her mother's story of how she'd forced Shannon's father to marry her when she found out she was pregnant, only to have him walk out on her four years later. It was her mother's excuse for not marrying again. Shannon didn't want to be making excuses.

Having decided she had to know how Clint felt, Shannon chased Clarissa out of the kitchen one afternoon. "Take the night off," she ordered. "I can finish up here."

"But Meessus Powell . . ." Clarissa protested.

"Go . . ." Shannon waved her toward the door. "I have a special surprise planned for Clint, and I don't want anyone around."

Clint parked his motorcycle in the garage and walked slowly toward the house. He wasn't sure how to tell Shannon what he'd done today. She was either going to love the idea or hate it. He hoped she loved it.

As he passed the bungalow, he noticed Clarissa in the kitchen. She waved, and he waved back. That she wasn't in the house was unusual at this hour.

Dusk was turning the leafless trees in the yard into eerie silhouettes, and a cold wind cut through his leather jacket. The back door banged when he shut it, and he was hit with a wave of heat. Quickly he took off his jacket and gloves and left them in the closet. Already the wool sweater he'd put on over his shirt felt too warm, and he was tempted to pull it off.

Food smells permeated the house, and the growling of his stomach reminded him that he hadn't eaten since breakfast. There hadn't been time with all he'd had to do: property to look at, papers to sign. The kitchen was where he headed, calling out Shannon's name.

"In here," she answered, and he detoured to the dining room.

The moment he stepped into the room, he understood why the heat was so high. The drapes were drawn, the lights were out and candles flickered on the table. Shannon stood by the chair he usually occupied at the table, the old waitress cap she'd worn at Mabel's on her head and an apron around her waist.

That was all she wore.

"Ah, Mr. Dawson." She nodded and smiled, and pulled back his chair. "My name is Shannon, and I'm your server tonight."

"So glad to meet you, Shannon," he said with a smile. The hunger he'd had for food disappeared, a new hunger taking its place.

His sweater came off, dropped to the floor, and he began unbuttoning his shirt as he walked toward her. "I was thinking of having some dessert."

"I'm sure we can find something that you would like," she said sweetly.

"I'm sure you can."

He had grown to expect the unexpected from her, yet he was constantly amazed. A man would never be bored by this woman, would never get enough of her. By the time he reached her, he'd pulled his shirt from his slacks. She spread it open, wrapping her arms around his waist and boldly drawing him closer.

"Our specials today are . . ." she began, and he chuckled. Her breasts were soft and warm against his skin.

"I think I know what I want."

"And what is that?" she asked innocently, fluttering her lashes.

"You." He took her mouth, silencing any further conversation with a kiss.

As their tongues entwined, he savored the taste of her, knowing he had missed kissing her, though they'd kissed just that morning and had made love the night before. Any time he was away from her he missed her.

Shannon's hands felt small against his back, her body tight to his. The need to explore consumed him, and he left her mouth to trail kisses down her neck to the deep valley between her breasts. Cradling them in his hands, he paid homage to each, kissing, suckling and laving her nipples with his tongue. He knew it was impossible, but her breasts seemed to grow larger, heavier, each passing day. He marveled at the perfection of her body and the fact that she had chosen him to love.

Lifting her apron, he plied kisses down her belly, feeling her tighten her muscles and experiencing a tightening of his own. "I've never made love to a waitress in an apron before," he said, and loosened his belt and pulled down his zipper.

"Does that mean you've made love to waitresses not wearing aprons?" she asked, her voice quavering as he kissed his way down to the juncture of her thighs.

He didn't bother to answer, and when she moaned in pleasure, he knew she didn't care.

She placed her hands against his head, but she didn't push him away or stop him. He knew how to please her, time and practice having taught him what she liked and how far to take her. It was when she gasped his name that Clint ceased his tormenting and stood.

His shirt went, and he pushed his slacks and briefs to his ankles, not bothering to take them off. Bracing her, he eased her back against the table, spreading her legs with his knees. He knew he should stop, should go upstairs and get the box of condoms in the nightstand by her bed. Only, he didn't want to stop, not now. They'd been lucky the first time they'd gone without protection. He prayed they were lucky again. Until he knew how she was going to react to his plans, he didn't want to start any babies.

Shannon tightened when he entered her, and he stopped, watching her face, afraid he was hurting her. Only when he felt her relax and saw her smile did he move. Closing his eyes, he focused on the feelings surging through him, every movement bringing him pleasure.

For three months he had feared she would tire of him, wake up and realize what she'd done. Every time she drove away, he was afraid when she came back she would tell him to go, that or she wouldn't come back, that a drunk driver would end his happiness or someone like his brother, who had no qualms about taking a person's life as well as her money, would steal from him the one thing he valued. Shannon would never know how many times he'd wanted to slip a tracking device into her purse, or follow her...to be there if she needed help. Old habits were hard to break, yet he knew he had to allow her to grow.

What he prayed was there was a way for them to grow together.

The tightening of her body brought his eyes back open. Her face was flushed, her eyes dark with emotion, and he knew they were together at the moment. They were shadow and light, the imperfect and the perfect. With her, he was poetic, brave and bold. She was his Roxane, and he would fight to the death for her.

A primitive rhythm pulsated within her, and opposites blended, each becoming whole.

Only when the wild beating of their hearts had slowed, did Shannon speak. "Coffee, tea or me," she said, grinning up at him.

He eased himself back. "I think I just took you."

"No thinking about it."

Which was true. When he was around her, he didn't think, simply reacted. To think, he'd had to get away, had had to spend time at the center, reevaluating what he wanted in life. It had taken three months. Now he knew.

He just hoped Shannon would share his dream.

Shannon watched him pull up his briefs and slacks. Suddenly chilled, she stooped down and grabbed his shirt. Slipping it on, she felt reassurance in its soft warmth and familiar scent. What wasn't reassuring was how Clint turned away from her, walking away from the table to stand by the buffet.

"We need to talk," she said.

"We need to talk," he said, at exactly the same time.

For a moment, she stared at him, then nodded. "You first."

"No, you first," he insisted.

She shook her head.

"I insist."

Again she shook her head.

Frowning, he shrugged and released a deep sigh. "Okay. I did something today. Something you may not like. Something that will take me away from here."

Shannon bit her lower lip, afraid she might cry. Saying nothing, she waited for him to go on.

"These past three months with you have been the happiest in my life, but I can't just live off your money. John is here, will always be here. I thought starting a security company was what I wanted to do, but when I began looking for places to rent, I realized going around and making people's homes safe wasn't how I wanted to spend the rest of my life."

He paused, and she knew she had to speak. "How do you want to spend the rest of your life, Clint?"

"Well, today I put a down payment on a farm out north of Sterling Heights. Actually I saw the place two months ago, but it's taken me some time to get assurance of a zoning variance. Today, however, everything was approved, in writing. They've agreed to everything I want."

"And that is . . . ?" she asked, feeling him slipping away.

"Well..." He came back and took her hands, bringing her to the chair he usually occupied and sitting her down. Then he pulled out another chair so he was facing her, their knees together, hers bare and his covered by his slacks. "What I want is to run a school of sorts, a place where Don can send the dropouts he feels have potential. Boys and girls. Men and women. People who need guidance and a helping hand. Right now he has five who would qualify. Two girls and three boys. These kids need to get away from the neighborhood, need to find out they're not stupid. They need to learn job skills, how to apply for a job, how to conduct themselves at an interview."

She didn't say anything, but he held up his hands. "I know. You're wondering how I'm going to pay for this school. And that is a problem. I'm using the money I saved to start a business to buy the farm, at least for the down payment. But I'll have to get donations. Don seems to think I'll find several corporations in the area who will give money if I can show the benefits of this program."

Shannon sat back, trying to absorb all he was telling her. Immediately he frowned. "Don't worry. I'm not asking you for any money. This is my idea, my gamble."

"And if I want to give you money?"

"I won't accept it."

She knew by the set of his jaw that there was no use arguing the point, at least not now. "What will you accept?"

"Well..." He hesitated, his fingers squeezing hers. "I guess that's up to you." He looked around the dining room, the candlelight flickering off the flocked wallpaper. "In my opinion, this is where you belong. John gave you everything. What I have to offer is work. No trips to Europe. No golfing every Tuesday and Thursday afternoon."

She didn't bother to mention she hadn't played golf for over three months. She was more concerned with what he was offering. "You want me to work for you?"

"No." He took in a deep breath, his chest expanding. Shannon held her own breath, waiting. Finally Clint spoke. "I want you to live there with me, as my wife."

As proposals went, she knew he could have done better. But then, he wasn't one to waste words, except when he wrote a love letter. She was glad she had love letters from him.

His fingers were tight around hers, and she knew he was waiting for her answer. She was tempted to prolong his agony, make him suffer with his insecurities as she'd suffered with hers the past three months. The concern in his eyes, however, got to her, and she smiled. "Sounds like we have a lot of work cut out for us."

It took him a second to realize what she'd said. His grin was immediate. "That's a yes?"

"That's a yes." As long as she was with him, the work wouldn't bother her. "Maybe I'll get my degree in education. Learn how to teach adults how to read. We could expand this, you know." And in spite of what he'd said, they would use the money she'd inherited. She couldn't think of a better use for it.

"I was thinking we might build a cottage for my mother there. I think I could talk her into moving away from the old neighborhood if she thought she'd be useful where she was going. I know one of the girls Don would like me to work with has a baby. Mom could watch the child while the girl was learning how to make a living."

"She could watch our baby, too, when I'm at school or busy," Shannon said, deciding it was time to tell him.

He nodded. "When we have one."

"How's April sound?"

Again, it took him a second to understand. She knew the moment he did. His gaze went to her belly. "You're pregnant?"

"You know me and some of those impulsive ideas I have. You wanted to be my protector, and I didn't want any protection."

"The first time we did it?"

She nodded, waiting for his reaction.

He touched her abdomen, slipping his hand under his shirt and resting his palm on her belly. She knew he couldn't feel any movement, but in a few more months he would. His dark eyes were wide when he looked at her. "When did you find out?"

"I took a home-pregnancy test in September. The doctor confirmed it two weeks ago."

"You waited that long to see a doctor?"

She shrugged. "I knew it wasn't going to go away, and I started taking vitamins, watching what I ate and drank. He said everything looks fine."

"And what I just did?" He glanced toward the section of table where they'd made love.

"No problem." She laughed. "This time it was safe."

"What am I going to do with you?"

"Love me," she said seriously.

"No problem."

His kiss was tender, cautious. She knew they would have problems. He was going to be overly protective, and she was going to be stubborn and impulsive, but she also knew they would work it out. The growling of his stomach reminded her that she was supposed to be serving dinner. Breaking away, she stepped toward the kitchen, but at the door she paused and looked back. "If it's a boy, what do you think of the name Cyrano?"

* * * * *

From the bestselling author of ASPEN

LYNN ERICKSON

NIGHT *Whispers*

Anna Dunning knows someone is watching her...stalking her. But she refuses to let fear change her life and she certainly doesn't want Mark Righter, an ex-cop with an attitude, tagging along as some kind of protector. But the stalker is getting closer—and now *he's* equally determined to remove Righter from the scene...and finally make Anna his own.

Look for *Night Whispers* in January 1997, wherever books are sold.

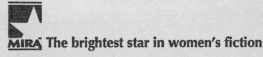

MIRA The brightest star in women's fiction

MLENW

Look us up on-line at:http://www.romance.net

Harlequin and Silhouette celebrate
Black History Month with seven terrific titles,
featuring the all-new *Fever Rising*
by Maggie Ferguson
(Harlequin Intrigue #408) and
A Family Wedding by Angela Benson
(Silhouette Special Edition #1085)!

Also available are:
Looks Are Deceiving by Maggie Ferguson
Crime of Passion by Maggie Ferguson
Adam and Eva by Sandra Kitt
Unforgivable by Joyce McGill
Blood Sympathy by Reginald Hill

On sale in January at your favorite
Harlequin and Silhouette retail outlet.

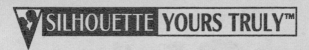
POP GOES THE QUESTION
by Carla Cassidy

A child's note, hidden in a balloon, inspires
Mary Wellington to secretly correspond with mommy-
seeking Annie Taylor. Then she meets father and
child in the flesh....

Thoughts on Annie: Cute as a button...and the kind of
daughter Mary could only dream of having.

Thoughts on Annie's Dad: Handsome as sin...and the
kind of husband Mary wanted more than anything. But did
she have what it took to make them the perfect family?

FOLLOW THAT GROOM!
by Christie Ridgway

Riley Smith thought he had the opportunity of a lifetime.
He would promote the grand opening of his honeymoon
hotel with a brand-new bride by his side. Unfortunately,
the bride-to-be split, leaving Riley searching for a willing,
last-minute replacement. Eden Whitney seemed more at
home with a book than a husband, but Riley could
overlook that. What he couldn't ignore, though, was the
transformation of his make-believe wife into a very real,
very desirable woman....

They were only together

For the Baby's Sake

Or were they?

Look for this heartwarming collection about three couples getting together for the sake of the children— and finding out along the way that it isn't only the children's needs they're fulfilling...

Three complete stories by some of your favorite authors.

BROOMSTICK COWBOY
by Kathleen Eagle

ADDED DELIGHT
by Mary Lynn Baxter

FAMILY MATTERS
by Marie Ferrarella

Available this February wherever
Harlequin and Silhouette books are sold.

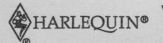 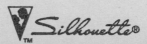